The Orange Slipknot

by
Jan Young

Illustrated by
Pat Lehmkuhl

Raven Publishing, Inc.
Norris, Montana, USA

The Orange Slipknot

Copyright © 2007 Jan Young

Illustrations and cover art © 2007 Pat Lehmkuhl

Published by Raven Publishing, Inc.
P.O. Box 2866
Norris, MT 59745 USA

This work of fiction is a product of the author's imagination. Any resemblance to any event or person, living or dead, is coincidental.

Manufactured in the USA

Library of Congress Cataloging-in-Publication Data

Young, Jan, 1951-
  The orange slipknot / by Jan Young.
      p. cm.
  Summary: Twelve-year-old Ben tries to be a responsible young man on the ranch where his father works, but repeated conflicts with the boss cause his father to doubt Ben's maturity, and he eventually realizes that it is up to him to do the right thing.
  ISBN 0-9772525-5-8 (pbk. : alk. paper)
  [1. Cowboys--Fiction. 2. Ranch life--Nevada--Fiction. 3. Conduct of life--Fiction. 4. Nevada--Fiction.] I. Title.
  PZ7.Y86524Or 2007
  [Fic]--dc22

                          2007010983

Author's Note

This book is for two groups of kids—town kids and country kids. Town kids will learn that cowboys are not just relics of the past or part of the rodeo world. For these kids, I have included a glossary of cowboy slang and ranching terms.

I also wrote it for country kids—the kids who are now my neighbors, who grew up on horses, whose dads are cowboys, who live on ranches—the kids who inspired this book.

This story is set in northern Nevada, part of the Great Basin area where cowboy culture and practices have been strongly influenced by the Spanish vaquero traditions. Cowboy culture varies throughout the different parts of the West. Terms used in this story might not be used in the same way in other western areas. Be sure to check the glossary for any words you don't understand.

Illustrations

Page 11 - *Ben kicked the ATV into gear and took off, leaving a roostertail of dust behind.*

Page 26 - *After measuring a new strap, he fitted the buckle to it.*

Page 51 - *5:30 Sunday morning*

Page 115 - *"I think I'll have me a little eye-winker."*

Page 138 - *A pool of blood formed slowly under Fred's head.*

Page 161 - *Ben and Skeeter tested the new riata on a few leppy calves in a pen down by the barn.*

Chapter headings - *Ben's orange slipknot, rather than a true slipknot, is a lasso made by tying a hondoo in one end of a piece of baling twine and threading the other end through it. It could "slip" and tighten around an object with a single jerk.*

Chapter One

Ben lay sprawled on his stomach in the alfalfa field when the Great Idea came to him. He jumped up, trotted over to the nearby haystack, and picked up some orange baling twine from a broken bale. Fashioning a slipknot in one end, he formed a small noose or lasso, then tied another piece of twine to the other end, making a long rope.

Ben approached a ground squirrel hole and arranged the loop over it. He lay down at the other end of his rope and whistled softly between his teeth. Soon a furry little head popped up, puppet-like. The dusty gray and tan of the squirrel's coat camouflaged it against the dirt as it stood up boldly, like a prairie dog, and peered around.

Yanking the rope swiftly, Ben took the slack out of it. His timing was perfect. The loop tightened around the squirrel's neck, catching one front leg, too.

With a whoop, Ben leaped to his feet. The squirrel hit the end of the twine like a wild horse caught in a lass rope. He bucked and twisted, squeaking with indignation.

"Whoa, there! Steady, boy!" Ben called, laughing gleefully. This was more fun than halter-breaking a colt! Leading his captive, he galloped toward the barn, shouting, "Dad! Look! He's broke to lead!"

Near the corrals, three cowboys stood talking beside their saddled horses. Inside the corral a few loose horses milled around. Two cowboys pushed a batch of bulls toward another pasture.

Ben's dad, Pete Lucas, holding a thermos cup of coffee, turned around. "Ben! No! Get back!"

It was too late. Ben skidded to a stop, but the squirrel galloped past him, hit the end of the rope, and chattering noisily, somersaulted right into the nearest horse.

The little black mare rolled her eyes, jumped forward, crowhopped, and pulled back. Her reins, draped across the fence, whipped over the board and fell free. As she stepped on them, she jerked her head up, and they snapped with a loud "pop."

"Let him go!" someone bellowed. Ben dropped the rope.

The squirrel leaped through the corral fence under the nearest horse. The twine rope wrapped around his hind foot as the squirrel dodged hooves.

The tall yellow horse kicked out. He bucked and snorted—then charged the fence. As the rope fell free, he took out the top rail with a splintering crash. Up and over, he led the way as the other horses followed in a blind panic. Cowboys, cussing loudly, tried in vain to stop them. One managed to snag the black mare with his lass rope.

Ben froze, his eyes wide. His stomach lurched. All the laughter drained out of him.

Hooves pounding, the runaways veered to miss a pickup coming down the long driveway. A wrinkled old face peered out the driver's side window. "What the...?" His well-dressed passenger turned to watch the loose horses thunder by.

Seeing the pickup, Ben gasped. "It's Fred!"

"Didn't I tell you to stay away from the barn today?" Ben's dad shouted. He swung into his saddle as he prepared to join the other cowboys in pursuit of the runaways.

Ben's face fell. "I forgot..." His voice trailed away.

"I heard you shooting—where's the gun?" demanded his dad as he unbuckled his rope strap and took down his lass rope.

Ben gulped. "Uh, I left it...in the field...I'm going to get it right now. I'm sorry, Dad." His heart hammered as he took off toward the pasture.

In the distance, the approaching bulls bellowed and began to scatter as the horses pounded toward them. A pickup door slammed, and a raspy voice growled, "Hey, where'd that kid go?"

"Oh shoot," Ben muttered. He raced to the hay-stack, grabbed his gun off a bale, and ducked out of sight. His heart thumped against his ribs.

Today started out so good, but I'm in deep doo-doo now. How could my Great Idea turn into a wreck like this? Chewing his lip, Ben thought back to the scene at the breakfast table, wondering where he had gone wrong....

Ben's fork stopped in mid-air, warm syrup dripping from the pancake. "But why can't I ride with you today, Dad?"

Pete Lucas wiped his mouth and took one last sip of coffee. "I told you yesterday," he said. "Fred is bringing a big cattle buyer who's flying in today. I don't want you anywhere near Fred!"

Ben hated Fred. The reason was simple—Fred hated Ben. He always had, ever since they moved here. Ben had no idea why. His dad was sure Ben was hiding some dreadful deed he'd committed against Fred. Since Ben couldn't prove that he wasn't, it gave him even more reason to hate Fred.

All the cowboys at the Circle A Ranch did what Fred said because he was the cow boss on the ranch. Fred was old and grouchy. He was so old and had worked there so long, he got the whole weekend off, instead of just Sundays like the other cowboys. But some Saturdays he had special jobs to do, like today.

"Why don't you do some target practice instead?" Pete suggested.

"Okay," Ben said, disappointed. This was his last Saturday to spend with his dad before school started on Monday. He loved working with his dad, even though sometimes he was hard to please. Ben wanted to cowboy on a ranch when he grew up and hoped that someday he would be as good a hand as his dad.

"What's the matter? You and that old gun aren't seeing eye to eye anymore?" Pete laughed. "Maybe I need to buy you a scope for it!" With a wink, he reached over and tousled Ben's hair.

His mother, Susie Lucas, smoothed his hair as she got up from the table.

"You guys!" Ben complained, grabbing his head with both hands. "Quit treating me like a baby!" His voice cracked momentarily.

"Baby?" Pete echoed teasingly. "It's that hair that I love! And those freckles on your nose!" As he reached for Ben's nose, Ben jerked his head away.

Getting up, Pete tousled Susie's short bouncy hair. "Just like this strawberry-blond I married!"

Ducking away, Susie said, "Can't you see I'm trying to pour coffee into your thermos?"

"Well, Ben and I have our morning planned. What's on your agenda, dear?" Pete asked.

"Oh, I need to finish preparing the piece I'm playing for church tomorrow. It's rather difficult. Then I have two piano students coming before noon."

Pete nodded as he stacked his dirty dishes in the sink. He pulled on his jacket. "Oh, and Ben..."

"Yeah, yeah, I know," Ben interrupted. "I'll remember to be careful with the gun."

As his dad headed out the kitchen door, Ben grabbed his jacket, the .22 that stood in the corner, and a box of ammunition from the shelf.

"Bye, Mom," he called as the door slammed behind him.

"Ben!" his mom yelled out the door after him.

He stopped and looked over his shoulder.

"What did you forget?"

"Sorry!" He ran back in, cleared his dishes from the table, and dashed out. A few seconds later, he jerked the door open again. Grabbing his hat, he crammed it onto his head and flew out the door.

Next to the shed sat Ben's brand-new, bright-red All-Terrain Vehicle. His grandparents had bought him the ATV for his twelfth birthday. He slid the rifle into the plastic tube attached to the utility box on the back rack and threw the ammo into the box. Ben jumped on and revved the motor. It sputtered

and died. Adjusting the choke, he turned the key
again.

The motor purred to life. "Udd-nn, udd-nnnn!"
Shivering in the brisk morning, Ben kicked it into
gear and took off, leaving a roostertail of dust
behind. August was over half gone, and in the
Nevada high desert, night-time temperatures
already dropped to near-freezing.

About a quarter mile down the dirt lane, Ben
skidded the four-wheeler to a stop, cranking the
handlebars so that it slid around in a half circle. As
a cloud of dust billowed up around him, he grinned
with satisfaction.

Three horses grazed in the small fenced pasture where he stopped. Ben reached through the
barbed wire fence and turned on the faucet above

the round aluminum water tank. A white mare and a splotchy, grayish-white gelding raised their heads to watch him. Off by himself was a tall bay. Nickering, he trotted over to join the others.

Although the ranch provided horses to each cowboy, most of them also had their own. These three carried his dad's brand on their right shoulder. It was a "P" with an upside-down and backwards "L" attached to the bottom of the "P." The ranch's brand was the same as its name, the Circle A—a perfect circle with a capital "A" in the middle.

Ben had learned to ride on the old mare, and she had taken good care of him. But Pete had finally decided that Ben needed his own horse. The young gelding, her last colt, belonged to Ben. Soapsuds, as they called the blotchy, mottled colt, wasn't exactly pretty, but he was Ben's first horse. Next spring, when he turned three, he'd be old enough to start under saddle. Ben dreamed of the day he'd finally be cowboying on his own horse.

"Hey, Soapsuds! How are you doing there?"

The colt eyed him curiously.

Ben sighed. "Just a few more months..."

Feeding and watering their horses every morning and evening was part of Ben's daily chores. There wasn't much grass left in the pasture, so they needed a little hay, too. Half a dozen bales were stacked near the fence. Ben pulled out his jackknife and slashed the three strands of orange baling twine on the top bale with a loud "pop...pop...pop."

The horses nickered as he grabbed a four-inch-thick flake of hay and tossed it over the fence. He pitched another a little farther down the fence and one even farther away. Soon each horse was tearing into its own flake, pulling it apart, and shaking it to loosen the firmly-packed hay.

While the water tank was filling, Ben picked up a brush lying in the weeds and crawled through the fence. As Soapsuds munched his breakfast, Ben brushed him all over, talking to him softly. When the water started to run over, he shut it off and crawled back through the fence.

Ben got back on the four-wheeler and roared down the road. Miles of dirt roads snaked around and through the ranch, and Ben took every chance he got to race up and down each one of them. Much later, he ended up at the alfalfa field across from the barn, a half-mile from his house. He parked near the haystack, far enough from the barn that there would be no danger of ricocheting bullets. He grabbed the gun and ammo.

Ben was pretty handy with the .22 his dad had given him for his ninth birthday. The old bolt-action gun had belonged to Grandpa Lucas before he died. Ben had spent many hours with his dad, learning to use it safely and responsibly.

His boots crunched through the weeds toward the target he had tacked to a bale. He filled the tube magazine with shells, slid it back into place, pulled back the bolt, and chambered a round. Hugging the worn wooden stock to his shoulder, Ben sighted down the barrel and clicked off the safety. He carefully squeezed the trigger.

"Crack!"

Not a bull's eye, but close. He fired again. He practiced from a standing position, then on one knee, and on his stomach, propped on his elbows.

Most of the ground squirrels had gone into hibernation, but a few were still out. One stood on the rim of its burrow, watching him. He aimed.

That's when it happened. That's when he got the Great Idea....

Now, here he was, hiding behind a haystack. *I am a dead man. They're all going to be after my butt— Dad, Fred, all of them. What an idiot!*

When the last of the cowboys had disappeared and Fred's pickup finally left, Ben slunk back to his four-wheeler. He emptied the gun, slid it back into the tube, started his machine, and made a bee-line for the house.

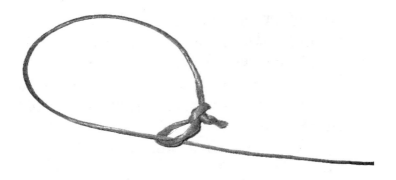

Chapter Two

At noon, when Ben joined his parents at the dinner table, he knew there was going to be a scene. Keeping his eyes down, he silently filled his plate and began to eat, waiting to hear what his punishment would be.

His dad opened fire. "Well, have you caused enough trouble today? Or what did you have planned for this afternoon?"

Ben didn't answer. *Why does Dad have to use that sarcastic tone? I hate that.*

"You've pulled some careless stunts before, but this takes the cake. Let's see...Skeeter's broken reins, a runaway horse which is still on the loose, and a bunch of bulls that have to be gathered for the second time." His voice rose. "Did you stop to think before you brought that berserk squirrel around the horses?"

Ben cringed. "No," he muttered.

"What? Look me in the eye when you're speaking to me," his father said sternly.

Ben looked up. His father's eyes were the same color of blue as his own, but sometimes they could be as hard as ice.

"No," he answered a little louder. "I didn't think."

Susie protested. "Pete, I don't know what this is all about, but that tone of voice is not necessary."

Ben flushed. He pushed his food around on the plate with his fork. Taking a deep breath, he said, "I'm *sorry*. Like I already told you, I'm *sorry*."

"You won't be seeing any of your friends for the next month, except at school. No company, no going to visit, no phone calls. You'll have plenty of time to learn to think before you act!"

Ben hung his head.

"As soon as you finish eating, you get your room cleaned up. It looks like a whirlwind hit it."

Ben got up.

"Then you spend the rest of the day shoveling manure."

That's not so bad. Cleaning corrals was one of his regular jobs.

"And you won't be getting paid for it for the next month."

"Aw, Dad!" Ben whined.

His father narrowed his eyes at him. Ben's eyes dropped. He cleared his dishes and slouched to his bedroom. He could hear his father telling his mother about the disastrous morning.

Ben turned on his stereo, cranked up the volume, and kicked at a pile of clothes on the floor. In a moment, boots clumped down the hall.

"Turn that down!" his dad yelled.

Ben obeyed, but made a face.

"And one more thing!" came the voice through the door. "Before you come home for supper, I want you to go apologize to Fred. He's *really* mad." The boots clumped back down the hall.

A couple of hours later, after his room finally passed inspection, Ben stood dejectedly at the scene of his disgrace. *Well, I'd better get these corrals cleaned. That'll give me plenty of time to figure out what to say to grouchy old Fred.*

The wheelbarrow stood on end against the side of the barn. The rake and the scoop shovel hung next to it on big nails. With a clang, Ben dropped them into the wheelbarrow and pushed it toward the gate of the corral. He stopped short. There in front of him, half covered in dirt, lay the orange twine.

The loop was enlarged and had obviously loosened and fallen off the squirrel as it ran. Ben couldn't hold back a mischievous smile. *It was pretty cool how I caught that little booger. Man, did he jump and flip!*

Sighing, Ben coiled the twine and stuffed it into his jacket pocket. He let himself into the corral and slid the latch into place. Half a day shoveling manure was definitely to be preferred to an hour or two of cleaning his room. Outside, life always seemed better. Ben loved the fresh air, even cold and crisp like today. The earthy smell of manure, the audience of horses, the bawling of cattle, and the rugged snow-tipped Ruby Mountains rising like a fortress above the ranch buildings were almost enough to make a person forget his troubles.

Ben raked up mounds of manure, then scooped them into the wheelbarrow until it could be heaped no higher. Working hard, he forgot about Fred. As he pushed the wheelbarrow toward the gate, the sight of Fred's truck brought him up short. It was headed his way.

"Aw, shoot!" he said to himself.

He set down the wheelbarrow and slid back the latch. Fred pulled up in front of him, shut off the motor, and rolled down his window. Ben pushed open the creaking gate and took a few reluctant steps toward the old man.

"Uh, Fred, I just wanted to say that..."

Fred never even heard him.

"There you are, you dad-blamed kid!" he yelled. "Do you know how long it took to get them spooky bulls rounded back up? And what about the horse that jumped that fence? He stepped in a squirrel hole and broke his dang leg!"

Ben's head jerked up.

"Broke his leg?" He knew what that meant.

"That's what I said, didn't I? He broke his leg!"

"I...I'm..." Ben stuttered. His stomach flip-flopped. He knew that a horse with a broken leg had to be put out of its misery. Only very valuable horses had their broken legs set.

"You killed that horse, boy! Guess it'll be coming out of your dad's pay. And I hope he whips the tar out of you!"

Ben slowly wiped a cold hand across his sweaty forehead.

"And those broken reins of Skeeter's, a good set of braided rawhide reins! Who's going to pay for that? I'll tell you who! You are, that's who! You're going to buy him a new set of reins!"

Ben bit his lip.

"I'm sorry, Fred," he said, talking fast. "I really am. I didn't know this would happen. I didn't mean to cause all that trouble." His voice was shaking. "I'll never make trouble again. I swear it."

"Yeah, sorry...You're always sorry about something. I never seen a sorrier kid than you."

Fred looked past Ben.

"HEY!" he yelled. "Those horses are coming out the gate behind you!"

Ben spun around and flapped his arms. "Git! Git!"

The horse nearest him wheeled around, eyes rolling. He careened into the arm of the wheelbarrow.

"Oh no," Ben groaned as the wheelbarrow, shovel, and rake tipped over. The four snorting horses raced around the corral, kicking and squealing. Ben closed the gate and latched it. He picked up the shovel and rake, righted the nearly empty wheelbarrow, and glanced over his shoulder.

Fred was climbing stiffly out of his pickup. As the shriveled-up old cowboy marched toward Ben, a slender border collie jumped out of the back of the truck and glided along behind his heels like a shadow. The dark look on Fred's face, under the brim of his battered, black felt hat, gave Ben an uneasy feeling.

"I've had it with you, boy," he growled, shaking a bony finger at Ben. "I've had it with your shenanigans. I been telling your dad that you're too young to be hanging around."

Seth, one of the cowboys, was trotting his horse toward the barn. At nineteen, he was the youngest hand on the outfit. Glancing at Fred, he reined his horse to a slow walk, pulled the brim of his hat down lower over his eyes, and rode on by.

"All you do is cause trouble! Every time you come around, you're bad news. You're plumb USELESS."

"But I promise! It'll never happen again."

"I've heard that story one too many times! The only reason I let your dad bring you around here is because he's my top hand. But no more, you hear? I don't ever want to see you around my barn and my horses again. Starting right now! Now git! Put them things away and get home!"

"But my dad told me to clean the corrals!"

"And I'm your dad's boss! And I said git!"

Ben pointed at the pile of manure. "Do you want me to…"

"GIT!" Fred bellowed. "NOW!"

The skinny little man turned and stumped angrily back to his pickup. Scowling at Ben, he started the motor and drove away.

The knot in Ben's stomach tightened. *So much for apologizing.*

Chapter Three

Ben slowly picked up the rake and scoop shovel. The energy he'd felt a few moments ago drained away. Leaning on the rake handle, he watched the horses as they milled around the corral. With a groan, he dropped the tools into the wheelbarrow and pushed it toward the gate. Even though it was empty, it seemed much heavier than before.

This time, he hurried through the gate and latched it behind him. He put away the tools and the wheelbarrow.

"Well," a teasing voice drawled, "if it ain't Bad-news Ben."

Startled, Ben spun around. Seth slouched against the tack room door, a crooked grin on his face, the reins of his sorrel horse in his hand.

Ben's heart sank. Seth was his best friend on the ranch. Or at least he had been up until now. Would this change everything?

"You know, I kind of like that name," Seth teased in his slow-talking way. He repeated it, emphasizing each syllable. "Bad-news Ben. It sort of fits you, somehow." He chuckled.

Ben turned slightly red. Seth *would* have to hear all that. "Hey, lay off, will you? I'm in big trouble around here. I'm not even supposed to *be* here."

"Don't worry, he's gone. Come here, kid," he said, with a jerk of his head.

Glancing in the direction Fred's pickup had gone, Ben obeyed.

Spurs clinking, Seth led his horse to the tie rack, where several unbuckled halters hung from knotted lead ropes.

"Come over here, Useless. Undo this saddle."

Though Seth was grinning, Ben's face burned.

He approached the sorrel's left side, tossed the stirrup onto the seat, and unbuckled the back cinch first. Meanwhile, Seth slid the headstall off, pulled the halter on, and buckled it.

As Ben finished pulling the long leather latigo strap from the cinch ring, the front cinch fell free. Seth went around behind the horse to the other side. He picked up the dangling front and back cinches and buckled their rings into a small strap attached near the horn. Ben reached down for the latigo, doubled it, and stuffed the doubled end up through the cinch ring. He let the stirrup fall back down.

Seth came around to pull the saddle off, but Ben said, "I got it."

He reached up and grabbed the front and back of the saddle and blankets. Hugging the heavy saddle to his chest, he stepped backwards. The right stirrup slid across the sorrel's sweaty back and fell, clunking Ben in the knee.

Seth followed Ben into the tack room, watching him slide the big stock saddle onto an empty rack while pulling the blankets out from under it. Ben turned the blankets upside down and laid them across the saddle, sweaty side up to dry. As Seth hung the bridle on a coffee can nailed to the wall above the saddle, he nodded in approval.

"There, see? You're not 'plumb useless.' You're pretty good help."

Ben just shrugged.

On their way out, each grabbed a brush from the plastic milk crate by the door. They brushed the horse's shiny red coat, one on each side of him.

Working around the horse calmed Ben. The smells of leather, manure, sweaty horses, and wet saddle blankets had always been a part of Ben's life. They were good smells.

He glanced at the ladder to the loft, one of his favorite places. He liked to explore among the piles of old harness and imagine he lived in the old days. *Guess I won't be playing up there anymore.*

Ben finished his side and dropped his brush in the milk crate.

"Put him up for me, would you? I've got to find a new chin strap for my snaffle."

"Sure."

Ben untied the rope and led the sorrel around the barn. He heard Seth rummaging through boxes.

He slid open the latch, keeping one hand on the gate as he let the horse in behind him. He shut the gate. He made the horse turn and face him before he removed the halter. Keeping the hind end pointing the other way would keep him from getting hurt if the horse playfully kicked up when he was turned loose. With the halter and a loop of rope hanging across his arm, he crawled through the fence and headed for the tack room.

"Thanks," Seth said without looking up.

"Sure," Ben said glumly.

Seth sat on an empty five-gallon bucket that he had turned upside down, a box of leather straps and scraps between his knees. "Grab a bucket."

Ben found one, turned it over, and sat down. Elbows on his knees, he propped a hand under his chin and watched Seth. The silence was comfortable. Finally Seth found the piece he wanted.

"Hand me my snaffle, would you?"

Ben reached for the headstall with the snaffle bit and rope reins and gave it to him. Seth dug his jack-knife out of his front pocket and cut off the frayed strap. He cut the little buckle off and tossed the old strap into the trash can. After measuring a new strap, he fitted the buckle to it.

"I think old Fred's got you figured all wrong," he said, not looking up from his work.

Ben thought on that. "But you're not old and grouchy like Fred." That brought a chuckle. "You're not even as grouchy as my dad. You're more like...a big brother."

"How would you know?" Seth teased. "You don't have one."

"But if I did...maybe he'd be like you."

Seth looked up at him, serious for a moment. Then with a twinkle in his eye he joked, "Flattery will get you everywhere, my boy."

Ben failed to laugh. "Well, it won't pay for that horse. Fred said he's going to take it out of my dad's pay." He got up and paced around the room. "Seth, my dad doesn't make much money."

Seth rolled his eyes dramatically. "Any man that will work for cowboy wages ought to have his head examined."

"Including you?"

Seth laughed. "We must be nuts—we spend all day looking at the south end of a northbound cow!"

Ben gave a half-smile. "Well, my dad's never cared much about money."

"Course not. He's here for the same reason as me and all the rest. We've all been bit by the same bug—we've got cowboy-i-tis." He shook his head. "It's an incurable disease, you know."

Ben turned and jammed his hands onto his hips. "This is not funny! I know it's my fault about the horse and all. I never meant for it to happen, but it's still my fault." He jutted out his chin stubbornly. "I couldn't care less about Fred, that old goat. But my dad..."

Ben's shoulders drooped and he sighed. "I got him in big trouble. He always says I'm his 'right hand man,' but I guess I really let him down."

"So, what are you going to do?"

"Well, I've been thinking." He stopped pacing. "I've got a little money in the bank. I can find some work after school and on the weekends. I don't know how much it'll cost, but my dad always says a man's got to take responsibility for his actions."

Seth began, "But you're..." He stopped.

Ben looked at him. "I'm what?"

Seth hesitated for just a moment. "You're right," he said, looking Ben in the eye. "You've got to take responsibility for your actions. That's not always easy. But I know you'll do the right thing."

Ben bit his lip. "How much do you think that horse was worth? And how much does a set of braided rawhide reins cost?"

Seth sighed and shook his head. "More than you'll be able to earn. Let's see. The horse? Maybe fifteen hundred. The reins—who knows? Skeeter made them himself." He snapped his knife shut. "Hours of hand labor go into a set of reins. Most cowboys can't afford to pay for that. That's why they learn to make them."

Ben swallowed hard. This was worse than he thought. He watched Seth hang up the snaffle and set the box back in a corner.

"Well, I'm headed into town, partner. You'd better skeedaddle on home before the old goat returns and finds you here. That would really be bad news."

Ben laughed briefly at the wicked grin on Seth's face. They parted company outside the barn, Seth heading for the nearby bunkhouse, Ben heading for his four-wheeler parked next to the corrals.

He wondered how soon his dad would be home. *I wish Dad was easy-going like Seth. Maybe he won't yell too much. I wonder if Fred told Dad about our "talk"?*

Shading his eyes from the afternoon sun, he squinted toward a puff of dust. There was his dad, riding toward the barn. Fred's pickup pulled up alongside him and stopped.

Ben gulped. *Oh, shoot. What's Dad going to say now?*

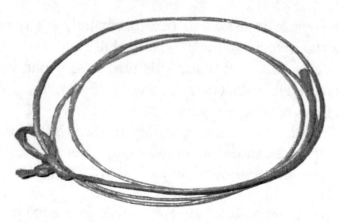

Chapter Four

Ben burst through the kitchen door, slamming it behind him.

"Mom!" he yelled. He raced into the living room. "Oh, there you are."

Susie was curled up on the couch with a novel. She looked up in surprise. "Ben! What's the matter? What's happened?"

Ben flopped into the large stuffed chair. "Oh, Mom, I've got to talk to you! I've got big problems!"

"Big problems? You mean worse than what happened this morning?"

"Oh, man, it just keeps getting worse!"

Rolling his eyes, he leaned his head back and slid down deeper into the chair. He grabbed its arms and spraddled his legs out in front of him.

He took a deep breath. "I went out to shovel manure like Dad said. And then Fred showed up. I tried to apologize, but he wouldn't even listen. He just ranted and raved about how bad I was."

Ben jumped up. Gesturing wildly, he talked faster and faster, running his words together. "I was standing there with the gate open and all the horses started to get out and he started yelling more and I shooed them back in and they tipped over the wheelbarrow and they were running all over the place and then he really started yelling..."

"Whoa there, calm down!" Susie interrupted. "Now sit down and tell me what he was yelling about."

Ben wilted into the chair. In a bitter voice, he said, "He went on and on about how I was irresponsible and always caused trouble and how I was useless. That's what he said, Mom. Useless."

Susie's eyes flashed. "Why, that old..."

"Mom, wait. That's not the worst of it. The horse that got away this morning—the one they couldn't find for awhile—he stepped in a squirrel hole and broke his leg."

Susie sucked in her breath. "Uh-oh."

"You're not kidding, uh-oh. They had to put him down. And Fred says I killed him. He says it'll come out of Dad's pay."

Ben waited for his mother to say something, but she only stared past him, biting her lip.

"Then he said he doesn't ever want to see me around HIS barn and HIS horses ever again. I told him that Dad said to clean the corrals, but he made me leave. Help me figure out what to do before Dad gets home!"

"Come to the kitchen with me," Susie said with a sigh. "I'm going to make myself a cup of tea. How about some cocoa?"

"Sure," Ben said glumly as he followed her.

He sat down at the table. "Mom, I've been thinking. I know Dad can't afford to replace that horse. And it was my fault and all. I've got that money in the bank, and I can earn some more."

She popped two mugs in the microwave and set out the instant cocoa mix and her favorite herb tea.

Ben drummed his fingers on the table. "I've got to earn some money right away, and school starts Monday! The only paying job I have around here is shoveling manure, and now I can't even do that! What am I going to do?"

Ben's eyes wandered over the framed photographs on the wall, pictures of his dad riding bucking horses back in his rodeo days. He had been on the college rodeo team in California. The money he won helped put him through school, but after he got his degree, he rimmed out for the sagebrush country, back to Nevada—just couldn't get cow-boying out of his blood. Once a cowboy, always a cowboy. Ben knew that someday his dad hoped to have his own ranch.

Susie finished fixing the tea and cocoa and sat down across from Ben. "Well, when I was a kid, we mostly babysat to earn money. Or washed cars, or baked cookies and sold them."

"Mom! I need a job! A real job!"

Susie frowned."Hmmm." She pursed her lips. "I could call around and see what I can find for you."

"No, Mom! I'm not a little kid anymore! I don't want my mommy getting me a job!" He ran his hands through his hair, mussing it up. His mom reached over and smoothed it.

Ben pushed her hand away. "Mom, stop! That's what I mean! You keep treating me like a little kid!"

Susie threw her head back and rolled her eyes. "Okay, okay!" She sighed. "What kind of work do you think you can get?"

"Well, some people are haying. I can rake or harobed. I'm a good driver, and I can make a pretty decent stack."

Susie looked doubtful. "I don't know.... Who were you thinking of asking for a job?"

Ben sipped his steaming mug of cocoa, thinking. "Maybe Mullens?"

"If they used you, you know they wouldn't pay you much."

Ben nodded.

"Have you thought about the...well, the transportation problem?"

"Uh, yeah, I've been thinking about that. Maybe I could get off the bus at someone's place, I mean if someone would hire me who happened to be on the bus route. Then you could pick me up when I was done. Or...maybe you guys would let me ride the four-wheeler to work and back? I'd stay off the pavement. There's plenty of room to ride down the side of the road on the dirt."

"Hmmmm," was all she said.

"I'm going to call right now and ask!" he said.

He looked at the valley's phone list on the wall. "Let's see—Carl Mullen." He dialed.

"Hi, Arlene? This is Ben Lucas.... Fine, thanks. How're you doing? Hey, I'm looking for a job, and I wondered if Carl needed any help, like with his haying?...Oh, he did?...Okay...Yeah, thanks anyhow. Bye."

He looked at the list and said, "He's got someone to help him. She suggested I try Mike Ellmore." He dialed again. "Hi, is Mike there?... This is Ben Lucas, and I wanted to talk to him about a job...Sure, I can hold on..." He whispered to his mom, "He's over in the shop...."

"Yeah, Mike, this is Ben Lucas. I wondered if you could use some part-time help, after school and

on weekends?...I can rake or harobed...You don't?...
Oh, she does?...I see, thanks anyhow. "

His mom looked at him questioningly.

"His wife helps him," Ben explained. "She does
a lot of work around the place." He frowned, scan-
ning the list. "I'll try one more." He dialed again.
"No answer," he said after a brief wait. "Shoot."

Ben cocked his head, listening. He peered out
the window and saw the pickup. "Here he comes,"
he said, his voice flat. He slumped into the chair.

As Pete came in the door, Ben glanced sideways
at his dad, trying to guess his mood.

Pete didn't look at Ben. He was quiet as he hung
his jacket and hat on the rack beside the door. Arms
crossed, Susie leaned against the counter, silent.

Pete poured himself a cup of coffee, pulled out
a chair, and sat down. Sorting absently through the
pile of mail lying there, he picked up a letter.

Ben felt hot and edgy. *This is worse than being
yelled at.* As Pete sipped his coffee and read, Ben
continued to steal glances at him.

"I see your folks are coming in a few weeks," he
said. At last he turned to Ben. "Fred told me about
the horse."

Ben felt the blood creeping up his neck and into
his face.

"He said you were screwing around at the
corral. He said you smart-mouthed him."

Ben exploded. "What? That's a crock of manure!

I wasn't screwing around, and I didn't smart-mouth him!"

Pete raised his voice. "Now don't go adding to your sins by lying to me about what happened."

"I'm not! I swear!" He gave his dad a detailed account of what had taken place at the corral.

Pete stared out the window, clenching and unclenching his jaw as he considered this information.

Trying to defend himself, Ben added, "Dad, I told you that Fred hates my guts. He always has, ever since we moved here. I don't know why. He's always after me about something."

"And I've told you not to lie to me! There's something you've been hiding—you must have done something!"

"Dad, I swear it! I'm not lying to you! How can I prove it?" he asked in despair.

"I admit that Fred is a grouchy old son-of-a-gun, but he's a good man, and I've always respected his word," said Pete.

"But Ben has never been one to lie to you," said Susie. "And I can't really imagine him smart-mouthing Fred, or anyone else for that matter."

"And you're always sticking up for him!" Pete retorted. "I'm trying to teach the kid some responsibility!"

Ben thought this might be a good time to bring up his idea. "Uh, Dad, about the horse..."

Pete didn't look at him or change the expression on his face. He just took another sip of his coffee.

Ben took a deep breath and plunged ahead. "Fred told me he's going to take the money out of your pay. I know we don't make much money, and it was my fault and all, and I'm going to pay for it myself." There was no use in mentioning the fruitless phone calls. He paused. "Seth told me the horse was probably worth fifteen hundred dollars. I have some money in the bank, and I'm going to get a job and earn the rest."

There! he thought, relieved to get that taken care of. *Now maybe Dad won't be so mad at me.*

Pete looked directly at Ben, an incredulous expression on his face. "You'll never come up with fifteen hundred. You'd be lucky to scrounge up five hundred."

Ben jumped to his feet, his eyes flashing. "Well, I'll show you! I'll prove you're wrong! I'll earn it all!"

He eyed his mother. "How long 'til supper?" he demanded, still angry.

She glanced at the clock. "About an hour and a half."

"I'll be over at the bunkhouse." He grabbed his jacket and stomped out the door. *Why does my dad have to be like that?* He brushed tears from his eyes.

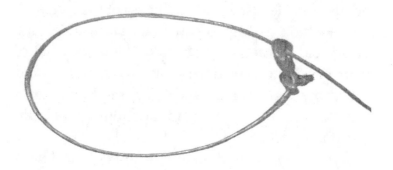

Chapter Five

Ben rode his four-wheeler to the bunkhouse on the other side of the barn, where the unmarried cowboys lived. He loved riding it. He rode it all over the ranch. As much as he had always enjoyed riding his bike, it had become a thing of the past, a relic of his childhood.

Parking alongside the mud-spattered pickups, he headed for the door. Several border collies and a Queensland heeler got up to sniff him and give a dutiful "woof." Boisterous talking and laughter inside was accompanied by country western music. As he was about to knock, Ben heard his name and hesitated. He listened.

"Did you see that look on Ben's face when that critter lit on my horse's butt? He like to died!"

"Talk about white, now that kid turned plumb white!" Ben heard hoots of laughter.

"Why, that little mare of yours dang near turned inside out trying to get away from that thing! I'd hate to be riding her next time a kangaroo rat jumps out from under a sagebrush."

"Oh man, did you see Fred drive up? He was madder'n a frog on a hot skillet! Whooo-ee!"

Frowning, Ben rapped on the door. Boots thumped across the plank floor, and the door creaked open.

"Well, come on in, little buddy. We were just talking about you."

A tall, lanky cowboy named Reggie grabbed him by the shoulder and propelled him into the room. He had a beer in his hand—apparently not his first.

"You want a beer?"

Ben grinned.

"Red-gee," Seth drawled disapprovingly. "He's in enough trouble already."

Reggie bellowed with laughter and slapped Ben on the back. "Hey, Ga-BEE-ca," he yelled across the room, "get this here feller a pop! You want a soda pop?" he asked Ben.

"Sure," Ben said, nodding. *Mom would have a fit—this close to supper.* But he didn't care. Lately he couldn't seem to get enough to eat. Gabica, a swarthy middle-aged Basque, handed him an icy can. Often just calling him "Basco," no one ever used his first name. Lounging on a bunk, Alvin, a Paiute Indian, gave a welcoming nod.

Skeeter was sprawled in a chair at the table. He pulled out another, and Ben sat down, confused by what he'd just overheard.

"Well," Skeeter said in his solemn way. "That surely was some sort of bodacious wreck this morning, now wasn't it?" His handlebar mustache, suspenders, and scruffy hat gave him an old-timey look.

Ben didn't know if he ought to snicker along with the others or hang his head. "Yeah, a heck of a wreck," he agreed, taking a swig of his pop. "According to Fred, all I ever do is cause trouble."

He absently reached into his jacket pocket and pulled out the length of orange twine. While they talked, his fingers busily tied and untied various knots his dad had taught him—one of his favorite pastimes.

Reggie threw back his head, hee-hawed, and slapped his leg. "Yep, you've given old Fred some grief, that's for sure!" He guzzled a little more of his beer. "I still remember the day you knocked Fred's pickup off the jack. He was changing a tire and forgot to block the wheels after he jacked her up.

When you leaned on her, down she went! Boy, was he mad!" He added, "…not that you should have been leaning on it."

Ben grimaced, remembering. "I didn't mean to. I just didn't think that would happen."

"As I recall, that was pretty much what Fred said," Skeeter chuckled. Doing his best imitation of Fred, he roared, "You just didn't think, kid! You never stop to think!"

The others hooted at Skeeter's imitation. Ben felt his face grow hot.

Gabica nodded. "How about the day ol' Ben was driving the tractor with the front-end loader on it and that hydraulic hose busted? Remember, he had that one-ton bale way up in the air. When it hit the ground, ol' Fred jumped purt-near out of his skin. I thought he was going to have the Big One." He snorted with laughter. "I thought I'd bust a gut laughin'."

"But that could've happened to anyone," Ben broke in. "I didn't wreck it. I just happened to be driving it when it broke."

Skeeter observed in his sober voice, "Dang right, kid. Them things always seem to happen to you."

"And always when Fred's around," Ben muttered. "But this didn't just happen. This was something I did that was just plain stupid."

"Well," Reggie mused, "trying to halter-break a squirrel was kind of stupid, but it sure was entertaining!"

Ben shrugged his shoulders. "How can you guys laugh? Fred and Dad are about to wring my neck."

"Your dad's sore because you're his kid, and he feels responsible," Gabica explained. "And Fred's sore because...well, he's always sore about something. He's not happy unless he's got something to complain about."

The others laughed, nodding vigorously.

"Well, this time I guess I gave him something to complain about...like your broken reins and that horse they put down. Man, am I in trouble!"

Skeeter shrugged. "Hey, don't worry about the reins, kid. They were the first pair I ever made, and I never did like them very well."

Reggie slammed his empty can down on the table. "That gelding was the phoniest, onry-est knothead I ever rode! Did you see how he blew up when that twine got around his feet? He's had plenty of ropes around his feet before. You can't count on a horse like that. Ain't that right, Basco?"

Gabica agreed. "If he'd had any brains, he'd have looked where he put his big feet. That clatter-footed son-of-a-gun never did pay attention. No wonder he stepped in that hole."

Ben raised his eyebrows. "Don't you guys even feel bad about that horse?"

Gabica looked at Ben for a moment. "Well, sure, son. No one likes to see an animal die or to have to kill one. But you've got to face the harsh realities of life. A horse like that was going to get someone hurt. There's no point in getting all choked up about him."

"Why, that dirty, counterfeit son-of-a-buck like to killed me last year," Skeeter said. "Remember when he stepped in that badger hole at the branding? He came up bucking and threw me off right on my head, and then my knees came down and broke five of my ribs!" He snorted. "I wouldn't give you fifty dollars for that sorry pot-likker."

Ben gasped. "But Seth told me he was worth about fifteen hundred!"

"That's what Fred gave for him. He was a good-looking horse," Gabica explained. "Fred sure got jobbed on that deal."

"Well, he said he was going to take the money out of my dad's pay," Ben said. "He didn't exactly say how much money."

"Oh, it'll be the full fifteen hundred, I'll guarantee you that," Gabica said. "Fred's pretty tight with money."

Ben clenched his jaw. "Well, I'm going to pay for it myself. I told my dad I'd earn the money. I already have a little in the bank I can use."

Gabica raised his eyebrows and pulled up a chair. He straddled it backwards and rested his arms across the back of it.

"So you had a little talk with ol' Fred, eh?" he asked.

"He told me I have to buy Skeeter another set of braided reins, too. How much do you think that will cost?"

"Whooo-eee!" snorted Reggie. "Mucho dinero!" He rubbed his thumb back and forth across his fingertips, holding his hand out like he was waiting for someone to put some money in it.

Skeeter got up and clinked over to his bunk. He had a habit of never taking off his spurs when he came inside, and they clinked against the plank floor. He clinked everywhere he went. And he always packed a pistol. His real name was Huntley something, and he came from a wealthy family in New York City. But he liked to tell people he was raised on a ranch in Texas, and he spoke with a Texas twang. He was what other buckaroos called "pretty punchy."

Ben's dad said Skeeter kind of overdid the buckaroo thing. "He tries too hard to look like something out of a Charlie Russell painting. You don't have to wear your spurs twenty-four hours a day to prove you're a real buckaroo. What's important is, can you fork a horse and read a cow?"

Skeeter pulled a box out from under his bunk, clinked back to the table, and set the box down in front of Ben. It was full of pieces of leather and an odd assortment of unfamiliar tools.

"This is where you get a set of reins. All it costs is hours of work."

"Well, Fred says I have to replace them," said Ben with a frown.

"Hmm," said Skeeter thoughtfully, stroking his mustache. "I'll make you a deal. What I really need is a new riata."

Clinking over to his bunk again, he took down the coiled riata that hung on a nail on the wall.

"Look at this," he said, showing Ben the worn places on the braided rawhide lass rope. "This one's about had it."

He shook out the coils, letting it slide through the braided leather hondoo on the end to form a small loop. He swung it lightly over his head.

"Why do you use that?" asked Ben. "Why don't you just use a rope?"

"Most of the time I do. But I prefer a riata when we're branding. They're alive in your hand. Like throwing a rattlesnake. How'd you like to make me one?"

"Make you one?" echoed Ben. "How?"

"I see you're always dingin' with ropes and strings and knots," observed Skeeter, glancing at the twine in Ben's hands. "Would you like to learn how to braid leather, kid?"

"I...well...sure!"

"I've got a piece of rawhide that's already fleshed and de-haired," Skeeter explained. "I'll show you how to cut it into strings and braid it. And I've already got a hondoo for the end of it, so you don't have to make one. If you do that, we'll call it even. How does that sound, pard?"

Ben nodded with enthusiasm, enchanted with the idea of braiding a rattlesnake.

Skeeter's voice became dramatic. "I'd be proud to pass on to you one of the disappearing skills of the true buckaroo…. That is, if you're wanting to be a buckaroo. Maybe you're wanting to be some kind of citified dude when you're all grown up?"

Ben shook his head. "Don't worry. None of that city stuff for me. If you'd take the time to teach me, I'd sure as heck like to learn."

Reggie grabbed his can and raised it high in the air, shouting, "To the last of the true buckaroos!"

Ben laughed at their antics, but after a moment he looked around glumly. "Well, I still have to come up with the money for that horse."

"How are you planning to do that?" Gabica asked.

"School starts Monday, but I'm going to see a couple of neighbors tomorrow about working after school and on weekends." Several heads nodded. "I'm hoping someone will hire me to rake or harobed for third cutting," he said, more confidently than he felt.

Skeeter cleared his throat. "Well, don't get your hopes up. Most folks have their haying crew already."

"I know a better job," came a voice from the corner of the room. Everyone turned to look at Alvin. He didn't talk much, but when he had something to say, the others listened with respect.

"Before I came here, I trapped pocket gophers. I still have traps. You can make pretty good money."

Ben got up and walked over to Alvin's bunk. "Really? How much do you make? How hard are they to catch?"

Alvin spoke slowly and deliberately. "Not hard if I show you. You charge a dollar a gopher. You pay me five cents of every dollar you make to use my traps. I have a hundred traps, but you can only set about thirty in the morning before school. Maybe fifty on the weekend, more if you want."

"Before school?" Ben echoed.

"When the sun comes up, you've got to be in the field. You can set maybe thirty traps in an hour, before school. Run them in the afternoon, reset them. Thirty traps, thirty dollars. Every day. Fifty traps on weekends, fifty dollars."

"An hour before school? Oh man," Ben groaned. "I don't know."

"You want to make money or not? Everyone around here has too many gophers. They ruin alfalfa fields," Alvin said.

Ben nodded. "I'll think about it. Thanks."

"Be here at daylight tomorrow. I'll be up."

"On your day off?" Ben asked, his eyebrow raised.

Alvin smiled his slow smile. "I'm always up early. I like to watch daylight come. If you can't get up early, don't be a buckaroo."

Sighing, Ben said, "Well, if you can get up that early, I guess I can too. I'll be here."

They played cards until Ben's dinner time.

"When can you start that riata?" Skeeter asked as Ben headed out the door. "How about Monday night?"

"Sure," Ben said. "Thanks. How long do you think it'll take?"

"Depends on how quick you catch on. If you work on it every night, not long. A few weeks."

"Okay. Well, see you in the morning, Alvin." Ben drove home, his heart light. His money problems were solved.

Chapter Six

That evening Ben got out his calculator and figured how much money he could make trapping gophers. If Alvin was right, he could make thirty dollars a day and fifty on Saturdays and Sundays.

What if he could run all one hundred traps on the weekends? Then he could make a hundred dollars on each of those days! He should be able to make at least $250 a week. So, in a month he could earn $1000. With the $200 he had in the bank, he'd soon have the money for the horse.

Ben wanted to tell his dad the good news, but he decided against it. His dad always said, "Less talk and more action." *Better if I just surprise him with the money and see his reaction. He'll be so proud!*

Ben relished the thought of showing up old Fred. He'd see that Ben wasn't an irresponsible kid. He'd see that Ben could work like a man and take on a man's responsibility.

He set his alarm. Life no longer looked so bleak. He hit the sack, confident and content, and immediately fell asleep.

At 5:30 Sunday morning, Ben got up, fixed himself a quick bowl of cereal, then left a note for his folks saying where he'd gone. He knew the four-wheeler would wake them, so he rode his bike. The crisp morning air bit his cheeks and nose.

Outside the bunkhouse, Alvin was waiting for him. They climbed into his pickup and drove to one of the alfalfa fields. When they reached the barbed wire gate, Ben got out to open it, so Alvin could drive through; then he closed it behind them.

Ben knew the rules about gates. The first commandment was, if you go through a gate that was closed, shut it behind you, and if you go through one that was open, leave it open. The second was like unto it in importance: whoever is sitting on the passenger side mans the gates. His dad always said, "The smart cowboy sits in the middle."

Alvin parked the truck and opened the tailgate. He had thirty traps, trap stakes, and a small shovel. He handed Ben a pair of canvas work gloves and pulled on his own.

Alvin picked up ten stakes and a trap carrier, a bent piece of metal rod with ten traps threaded onto it. He hadn't said a word. Ben wondered if Alvin was even going to tell him how to trap. Cowboys were like that. They expected you to watch and figure things out without asking a lot of dumb questions. So Ben paid close attention to every detail.

Carrying the shovel with the handle downward, Alvin began walking, looking at the ground. "The alfalfa's pretty tall. They won't be easy to spot."

The leafy dark green alfalfa stood about a foot and a half tall. The plants had been cut with the swather, about a month ago, and later baled into hay. It had been the second cutting of hay this summer. After third cutting the cattle would be rotated into this field to graze on the stubble that was left. September's freezing nights would end the high desert's growing season.

Alvin stopped and pointed with the shovel handle. "See this mound?"

Ben came closer and looked.

"It's not fresh," he said. "It's an old mound. The dirt is dry. You won't catch a gopher here."

Alvin explained how each gopher digs many tunnels, about eighteen inches underground. They seldom venture above ground except to push the excess dirt up out of the way. That's what makes the holes and mounds.

"Don't they have to drink?" Ben asked.

"No, they get their water from the alfalfa roots and leaves they eat. They fill their cheek pouches with roots and stash them in their nests. That's why they're called pocket gophers."

He pointed to a cluster of mounds. "See these workings? The females work in a circular area around their nest."

He pointed to some other mounds. "The males go in a straight line from nest to nest, looking for females to breed. See these mounds out this way?"

Alvin was the same way about dogs, horses, and cattle. He just seemed to know how they think.

"Wow!" Ben said with admiration. "How did you learn so much about animals?"

"I spend a lot of time watching them. I observe their habits. I like to think about them." He laughed a slow huh-huh. "I read books too."

They walked farther and stopped again. Alvin pointed. "This mound is fresh. See how the dirt's dark and damp? A gopher has worked here within the last few hours. I'll set a trap."

Alvin jabbed the shovel handle into the mound and exposed the hole. He showed Ben how to set a trap.

Ben picked up the shovel. "Now you watch while I try one."

"Okay," agreed Alvin.

Ben walked a little ways. "Here's a mound. I'd say it's not fresh. It doesn't look damp like the one you just set."

"Good," said Alvin.

Ben walked past several others. "Here's a darker mound. Shall I try it?"

Alvin held out his hand for Ben to wait. "See this part of the mound that looks rounded and lumpy like a cauliflower? That's where the hole is. Probe there, at an angle."

Ben obeyed and the shovel handle sank. He pulled it out and scooped the loose damp earth away from the hole. He felt clumsy as he followed the steps Alvin had showed him.

"You'll get quicker with practice," Alvin said.

Between the two of them, even as slow as Ben was, they had the traps set in an hour. They drove back to the bunkhouse.

"When you get home from church, we'll run your traps," Alvin told Ben.

"Okay. See you later," Ben said.

Before returning home, he fed and watered Soapsuds and the other two horses.

When Ben walked into the house, pleasant morning smells greeted him. A pot of boiled coffee simmered on the stove. Bacon crackled and sizzled in a black cast-iron skillet. Sourdough hotcakes browned on the griddle.

"I had some cereal," Ben told his mom, "but it's worn off already. I could use some more breakfast!"

She smiled and set another place at the table. Sitting down, Ben announced, "Alvin's been showing me how to trap gophers. He says it's a good way for me to earn some money."

Pete said nothing as he came to the table, but Ben didn't let it bother him. They ate a quiet breakfast and by 9 A.M. they were in the pickup in their Sunday clothes, headed for Elko, sixty-some miles away. Fifteen miles the other direction was their own little town of Greeley, where Ben went to school. All it had was a two-room school, a tiny post office, a bar and small store combination, and a community hall. A handful of homes completed the town. Everyone else lived out in the valley.

Shortly after 1 P.M.., Ben was back. They had grabbed hamburgers on the way out of Elko, so all he had to do was change into work clothes and ride his four-wheeler to the bunkhouse. Alvin was waiting.

Alvin looked over the four-wheeler, throwing a small coffee can into the box on the rear rack.

"This is a good trapping rig. Put your traps and stakes in here. This tube you carry your .22 in will hold the shovel. Drive it out to the field, and we'll use it to run the traps."

Ben followed Alvin's pickup out to the field. They grabbed shovels, gloves, and trap carriers and headed for the nearest trap. Alvin jerked up the stake and knelt down, carefully easing the trap out of the hole so as not to lose the dead gopher. He held it so Ben could see the gopher up close.

Short smooth grayish fur covered the thick muscular body, about eight inches long, with a hairless tail about four inches long. Ben touched the small round ears and the heavy claws on the front paws.

"Aw, he's so cute!" Ben said.

"Always wear gloves. A live one in a trap will bite you. Ever seen two gophers fight?"

Ben shook his head.

"Pretty vicious," Alvin warned. "See his long curved front teeth? They never stop growing. If he didn't gnaw roots, they would curve right around into his throat."

"Oh, gross!" Ben said, laughing. The yellow protruding incisors made the gopher appear buck-toothed, like a girl Ben once knew.

Alvin poked the big fur-lined cheek pouches, showing Ben the chewed-up plant matter inside.

"How do they get it out?" Ben asked.

"They squeeze the pouches forward with their paws, then turn them inside out and clean them," Alvin explained. "They are pretty clean, for a rodent. They even have a bathroom in their nest."

"You're kidding!" Ben exclaimed. "How do you know?"

"I've dug down and followed their tunnels. There's a nest where they store their groceries, and another chamber full of manure."

He poked the shovel handle down the hole and rotated it, opening the hole and exposing a slanting vertical shaft. He talked as he dug. "There are different kinds. These big ones are Townsend's pocket gophers. They're only found in the Great Basin."

He showed Ben where the shaft leveled off into a deeper horizontal tunnel.

"If these fields were flood irrigated, the tunnels would fill with water and kill the gophers. But here, everyone uses sprinklers."

Ben looked at him in surprise. This was the most he'd ever heard Alvin talk. He never realized Alvin was so smart. He tried to picture him in school.

"Did you like school?" Ben asked.

"No, I hated it," Alvin said, laughing his huh-huh. "I wasn't interested in that stuff."

"Well, you sure know a lot," Ben said.

Alvin grinned. "I like to learn about stuff that interests me."

Removing the dead gopher, he dropped it in the hole and threw the trap and stake into the box on the back of the four-wheeler. He pulled a pair of wire cutters out of his back pocket, cut off the tail, and dropped the gopher back in the hole.

"Why'd you cut off his tail?" Ben asked.

"You turn them in for proof of your count. One gopher, one tail. Keep the can in your freezer." Grinning, he dropped the tail in the can. "I used to throw the dead gophers in buckets. I gave them to the rancher. One guy kept the buckets in the back of his truck." Alvin's shoulders shook in a silent laugh. "It was real hot. He forgot to take them to the dump. They all rotted."

Ben's mouth twisted. "Oh, yuck!"

Alvin nodded. "Better to leave them here for the crows."

Alvin got on the four-wheeler and drove to the next stake. Ben trotted after him.

"This trap hasn't been set off. You would leave it here until morning. Then if it's still empty, pull it and reset it somewhere else." He pulled it up. "I'll take it out since we're just practicing." He pointed to the four-wheeler. "Now you pull all the traps." Ben took off, and Alvin walked back to his pickup.

Ben finished running his traps. On the way home, he realized that it was time to go ask someone for a job. *I don't even have any experience doing this. What if no one wants to hire me?* Icy fingers of doubt wrapped around his stomach.

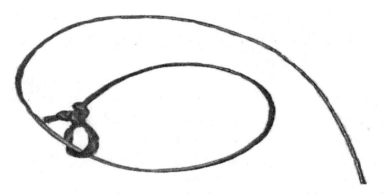

Chapter Seven

"Mom, can you drive me to the neighbors to ask about trapping jobs?" Ben asked. "That is, if you're not too busy?"

Susie sat at an old battered desk in the kitchen, working on Ben's computer, a birthday present several years ago from his grandparents who lived in California. They had been worried that living out here in the Nevada sagebrush, far from civilization, deprived Ben of opportunities that city kids had. A computer would help him to fit into "life in the real world," as his grandpa often said. Ben used it for homework and playing games. They couldn't afford an Internet connection, though, since even a call to Elko was long distance.

Ben had talked his mom into learning how to use the computer, too. Having studied accounting in college, she worked part-time keeping books for the ranch and was learning to use the computer in her accounting.

Susie clicked out of her program and turned the computer off. "This thing is giving me a headache. Some fresh air is just what I need. Anyway, I have some things to drop off at the mailbox."

As they went out the door, Ben asked, "May I drive?"

"No!" his mother said indignantly.

"Aw, Mom, Derek's folks let him drive on the road."

"Well, I'm not Derek's folks, and you don't need to be driving on the road."

"It's not like there's ever any traffic on our road. You know we won't even see another car."

She shot him an exasperated look.

"Just to the mailbox, then?" he wheedled, conjuring up his sweetest pleading smile.

His mom laughed and headed for the passenger side of the truck. "You're a pest!"

Ben grinned. *One of these times I'll wear her down.*

Like most local kids, Ben had been driving for several years already. He drove around the ranch and on the dirt roads out through the sagebrush. He often drove alone in the old work truck to visit Derek, an eight mile run out the back way on dirt roads. His folks didn't let him drive alone in the good truck.

He headed up the three-mile-long driveway. There were two barbed wire gates to go through before they got to the road. When Ben drove, his mom or dad had to open and shut the gates. That was the rule, he always reminded them, and it amused Ben immensely. It made him feel grown up.

At the pavement, he stopped and changed places with his mom. She got out and pulled up the home-made lid on the white-painted barrel that served as their mailbox, dropped her envelopes in, and put up the red flag.

The barrel sat on its side, supported by two fence posts. Big enough to hold large packages, it saved them lots of trips to the post office. Everybody on the Circle A got their mail here, each in their separate mail sack. On both sides of the barrel was painted the ranch's brand.

Asking someone for a real paying job was a new experience, and Ben felt more than a little nervous. It was so important that he get a job. Their first stop would be Barlows, their closest neighbors about three miles down the road.

There were no houses between their ranches, only endless waves of dusty gray-green sagebrush. A few scattered cattle grazed on the bits of dry grass that grew among the sagebrush. Most of the cattle were still up on the mountains. From its perch atop a power pole, a golden eagle watched them go by.

As they drove down the valley, Ben saw several ranches in the distance along the base of the majestic Ruby Mountains, which rose abruptly from the high-desert valley floor. Each ranch, marked by a cluster of cottonwood trees, sat below the mouth of a small canyon, where yearly snowmelt formed the spring runoff that watered their fields and meadows.

The Circle A sprawled at the mouth of Horse Canyon. The creek that drained Horse Canyon was known as Horse Creek (and was pronounced "crick" rather than "creek," as Ben always informed their city visitors). This time of year, Horse Creek was dry.

Susie drove through Barlow's ranch yard, past a set of corrals and two houses. The grandparents, who had homesteaded the ranch some sixty years ago, lived in one. John, Shirley and their three little kids lived in the other. Many ranch families in the area, like this one, consisted of three generations.

Seeing John Barlow working on his bale wagon in front of the shop, Susie drove over and stopped. As Ben opened his door, she opened hers.

"Mom?"

She stopped.

"I'd rather go by myself."

"Oh," she said, giving Ben a sideways glance. With an understanding smile, she shut her door.

Ben got out and tried to look casual, but mature, as he walked up to his neighbor. "Hi, John."

John looked up. "Hey there, Ben, what are you up to?" he asked agreeably.

"Not too much. What's wrong with your harobed?"

"Oh, just a broken bolt."

He leaned further over the machine, grunting and muttering. "Dirty rotten pot-likker! Can't quite reach it. Grab that pair of needle-nosed pliers there, will you?"

Several tools were lying on the ground. Ben handed him the pliers, but John didn't take them. "Just reach those right in here and pull this piece back out of the way."

Ben pulled and watched John extract the offending bolt.

"There!" John grinned with satisfaction. "Thanks. You came along at just the right time."

Ben cleared his throat. "John, I'm looking for a job."

"Oh, are you, now?" John straightened up, crossed his arms and leaned back against the bale wagon. "What kind of a job?"

In his most business-like voice, Ben said, "Well, I understand you have a gopher problem. I was thinking maybe I could trap your fields for you."

John took off his glasses, pulled a bandanna out of his back pocket, and began polishing them. Ben waited for him to speak.

"You're right about the gophers," said John finally. "I had some high-powered trapper come in here about three years ago and got them pretty well under control. But the dirty sons of guns have come back as bad as ever." He put his glasses back on, folded his bandanna, and stuffed it back into his pocket.

"I charge a dollar each, and I can set thirty to fifty traps a day," Ben said, trying to sound more confident than he felt.

"A dollar apiece?" John started picking up his tools.

Ben wondered if he'd asked too much—or too little.

"Well, that hot-shot trapper charged me $1.50 at 100 to 200 gophers a day. That cost me a pretty penny. I like your price a lot better."

Ben's hopes soared.

"You've got yourself a deal, young man. See that pivot over there? Start in that field."

He pointed out the field in question, a huge circle of alfalfa—137 acres, to be exact—with a long, wheeled sprinkler stretching across the radius of it. Several other pivots adorned the fields around it. They were called center pivots because they pivoted around a control tower at the center.

"Thanks, John." Ben stepped forward and stuck out his hand like his dad had taught him. John smiled and shook Ben's hand. "I'll be here at sunup tomorrow."

Ben set his alarm early for the first day of school, getting up the same time his folks did. He tossed his lunch and backpack on top of the traps in his box and left on the four-wheeler, stopping first to feed and water the horses. When he reached the road, he noticed a pickup go by with its headlights on. The sun wasn't up yet. To be safe, he turned on his lights too, even though he'd be staying on the side of the road.

His helmet provided a little protection from the chill wind as he drove down to Barlows. After setting his thirty traps, he drove up to the road to catch the school bus. He parked by Barlows' mailbox and stashed the key in his pocket. Although the bus didn't usually pick anyone up at this road, it stopped when Ben waved. He handed the driver the note his mom had written, giving him permission to get on and off the bus at Barlows.

Ben headed for the back of the bus, where the oldest kids always sat. He plopped into the long back seat by Derek and James as the bus lurched forward.

"What are you getting on here for?" Derek asked, as Ben knew he would.

"I've got a job," Ben answered nonchalantly.

"I've got to set my traps before school, and I'll get off here to run them in the afternoon."

"That's lousy hours," Derek said. "But good money. When I trapped for Smiths, I made a couple thousand for the summer."

"No kidding?" Ben exclaimed.

"What a crock," James said. "My dad makes me trap our fields, and he won't even pay me. He says I ought to just be happy to do my part around the place to earn my keep or something."

"Yeah, right!" Ben and Derek laughed.

"But at least your dad lets you drive his old pickup to the bus," Ben said. "I keep begging my dad, but he says I should feel lucky to have a four-wheeler to drive."

The bus arrived at Greeley, drove past the store and the post office, and pulled into the yard of the two-room schoolhouse. The boys headed for the upper-grade room, which the thirteen fifth-through eighth-graders would share this year.

Ben found it hard to keep his mind on school, what with being mad at Fred and excited about his job and all the money he was going to make. Although he was a good student, he was not an indoor kind of person. He was glad when he was back at Barlows.

As he got off the bus, Ben strutted with pride. Having a job was a great feeling, and his beloved four-wheeler awaited him. He fished the key out of his pocket and grabbed the handlebars as he threw a leg over.

He inserted the key, turned on the ignition, and pressed the starter button. Nothing happened. He tried again. Nothing.

"Dang it all!" Ben switched off the headlights he had left on that morning. "How could I be so stupid?"

It was a long walk to the Barlows' house. Ben found John in the shop, welding on his tractor.

"Excuse me."

John turned off the welder and took off his welding helmet.

"Sorry to bother you." Ben's face flushed with embarrassment. "Um, I've sort of got a problem," he said awkwardly. "I've got a dead battery on my four-wheeler. I left my headlights on this morning. I need a pull-start."

This is so humiliating. What a way to start a job. He must think I'm a real dolt.

If John was put out, he managed to hide it. "I've got a tow rope in my pickup," he said. "Come on. We'll have you running in a jiffy."

They got in John's truck and drove out to the road. John pulled up in front of the four-wheeler. Ben got out and reached in the back for the heavy rope. He quickly knotted one end to John's trailer hitch and the other end to his grill. He climbed on, shifted into neutral, and nodded. John pulled slowly ahead until the rope tightened, then drove off.

Ben shifted into gear and soon heard the familiar "udd-nn, udd-nn!" He waved John to a stop, then jumped off, untied the rope, and threw it back in the truck. He silently thanked his dad for all the times he had made Ben help pull-start a dead truck. It would be even more humiliating if he didn't know how.

"Thanks, John," he called.

John nodded. "You bet." He smiled as he drove off.

As all the traps with gophers in them were pulled, Ben reset them further down the field. He put the tails in a sandwich bag—they'd go in the can in the freezer that evening. Every so often he glanced at his watch, then toward the road. Sure enough, there went his mom on her way home, right on time. On Mondays, Wednesdays, and Fridays, she delivered mail to the next valley over. There was no town or post office there. The few scattered ranches were too remote for the regular mail delivery.

Her mail route, bookkeeping, and some piano students helped with the bills, especially since they were making payments on the surgery she had a few years ago. Most ranch jobs didn't provide health insurance. Sick leave and paid vacation were unheard of. Ben knew his folks struggled to pay bills, which was one more reason he wanted to pay for the horse himself.

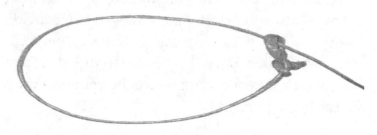

Chapter Eight

As he drove in from the field, Ben saw John standing on the porch steps. John waved him over, so he pulled up and turned off the motor. Shirley was setting a tray on the picnic table inside the closed-in porch. Their three small kids grabbed snacks and headed for the lawn. John held the door open, and Ben walked in.

"Well, how was your first day of trapping?" John asked. "Here, come sit down, and we'll have us a bit of a snack." They all sat down at the table.

"Did you want to, er, wash your hands?" Shirley asked hesitantly.

"Naw," Ben said, grinning. He reached for a cookie. "I had gloves."

She raised her eyebrows and shrugged. "So how many kids are there in the school this year?"

Ben thought a minute. "Oh, about twenty-nine. We don't even have any sixth-graders in my room."

"Well, I was so happy when John told me he hired you," Shirley said, handing him a mug of hot cider. "He's always after me to go out and set a few traps every morning, and I just don't have time. Of course, I never get paid for it, either," she added, laughing.

"So. How did it go?" John asked.

"Well, I caught pretty good—I think I'll have thirty by morning."

"Those mounds of dirt get baled up into my hay bales," John said, waving his hand toward the field, "so I can't get a decent price for my crop. Cows just don't like to eat hay with dirt in it."

Ben laughed. "I can't say that I blame them."

"All that dirt ruins the blades on a swather. Eventually, the gophers eat so many roots that the crop just shrivels up and dies. Why, I know ranches that have actually gone under because of gophers. They went bankrupt."

"Wow," Ben said. "That's awful." He shook his head slowly.

"Yeah, it's tough to make a living farming, what with gophers, squirrels, weeds, and fuel prices keep going up...then there's all the dang government regulations..."

"Now, John," Shirley interrupted. "Don't get on your soapbox. I don't think Ben wants to hear your views on politics."

Ben laughed and got up. "I'd best get going. Thanks, Shirley." He gulped the last few swallows of cider and set his mug down.

Riding home, Ben noticed how cool the afternoon was for this time of year. *Things are looking up. I'm not only making money, I'm helping John and Shirley keep their ranch going.* That made him feel pretty good. *Happy as a gopher in soft dirt,* he thought, grinning at his own joke.

When Ben got home, he settled down to his homework, so his folks wouldn't mind his spending the evening with Skeeter. After dinner, he showed up at the bunkhouse for his first lesson in the art of riata-making.

Seth let him in. With a big grin he announced, "Hey, look who's here! It's Bad-news Ben!"

Ben grimaced as he came in but took the ribbing in stride. The others gave Seth a blank look, so he had to explain about what he overheard between Ben and Fred.

"Well, pull up a chair, Bad-news," Skeeter said with a twinkle in his eye, "and let's see how much damage you can do to a piece of leather." He clinked over to his bunk, pulled out the box and a rolled-up hide, and clinked back to the table where Ben sat.

Skeeter dug around in the box and pulled out a dowel—a short, thick, round wooden peg with a razor blade and a nail sticking out of one end of it.

"What's that?" Ben asked.

"We're going to slice this rawhide into braiding strings. You hold the dowel under the hide, like this, and pull the hide around slowly with your other hand." He demonstrated. "Keep the edge against this nail, so the string is the right width."

He let Ben try. "Uh-oh," Ben said. "Mine doesn't look as even as yours."

"Hold it more like this," Skeeter said, guiding Ben's hands. Ben's strip became more even, the longer he worked.

"How was your first day trapping?" asked Alvin.

"Not too bad," Ben answered, "I'll know tomorrow morning when I pull all my traps."

"Any problems?"

Ben didn't answer for a moment. The dead battery incident was better left untold. "Nope."

"Ben the Gopher Getter!" Gabica joked. "Killing gophers to make amends for killing a horse. That's kind of funny, isn't it?"

Ben's mouth dropped open, but nothing came out. He hadn't thought of it like that. And it didn't seem funny at all. "That's not what I..." he began, then his voice trailed off.

"Lay off him, he's just a kid!" Seth said, his voice sharp. "Hey, don't get the wrong idea," he said to Ben in a gentler voice. "No one likes to kill things.

But sometimes you have to...to eat, or to protect yourself or someone or something, or to put a wounded animal out of its misery."

"You mean, like shooting that horse that broke his leg?" Ben asked.

"Yeah," Seth said. "Exactly. Would you have shot him, or would you let him lie there and suffer because he was too pretty to shoot?"

Ben bit his lip. He didn't like to think about having to do that. It would be hard.

"No one likes to," Seth explained, "but it's either that or watch him suffer and know you can't help him. It was the only humane thing to do."

"Yeah," Ben muttered, looking at his watch. He was relieved to have an excuse to change the subject. "I don't think I'm going to get this done tonight. Can I quit here and finish it tomorrow night?"

"Sure," Skeeter said. He rolled up the string and the dowel into what was left of the hide.

Ben rode home, pulled up in front of the house, and turned off the motor. He sat awhile and gazed at the clear star-studded sky. He could hear his mother playing the piano...the familiar strains of "How Great Thou Art."

He had grown up hearing the old hymns—at church and at home. He hummed along, hearing the words in his head. *O Lord my God, when I in awesome wonder consider all the worlds Thy hands have made...*

The pungent smell of sagebrush and the sweet aroma of the nearby haystacks were intoxicating. *I see the stars, I hear the rolling thunder, Thy power throughout the universe displayed...*

A horse snorted and stamped, a few cattle bawled in the distance—the background music he had grown up with. Their music blended with his mother's music, like melody and harmony.

Then sings my soul, my Savior God, to Thee. How great Thou art, how great Thou art! He felt quiet inside, like being in church.

Being a buckaroo and having his own ranch someday was his dream. In his mind, he saw himself riding a good-looking cow horse that he had trained. Driving a herd of slick, fat, white-faced cattle up into the Ruby Mountains to summer pasture—cattle wearing his own brand. Putting meat on his family's table—beef that he had raised himself. Producing food that would be eaten by hungry people all over the country. Being his own boss. Beautiful dreams.

Now the music changed. The eloquent strains of Beethoven's "Fur Elise" floated in the dark— notes so sad and beautiful that Ben ached inside. Somehow a shadow had fallen over his dream. Unpleasant thoughts about money, ranches going under, horses having to be shot. Was this life in the real world?

Maybe Grandpa and Grandma are right. Life might be better in the city—easier, more pleasant.

He could imagine what his dad would say if he ended up living in a city, working for some big company, wearing a suit, carrying a briefcase. He'd never hear the end of it, no matter how much money he made. His dad had rejected that lifestyle. He had chosen to live out here, even though they didn't make much money and probably never would.

Money isn't everything, his dad always said. Instead of money, they had wide open spaces, clean air, knew everyone for miles around, and never needed to lock the house or the pickup. One of his dad's favorite sayings was, "The only good thing about those towns is they keep all those dang people out of the country."

The music faded away. Then Seth's voice echoed in his head. *He's just a kid.* Ben scowled in the darkness at his tangled feelings.

Chapter Nine

Before school the next morning, Ben drove to Barlows, hunched over against the cold. He pulled all his traps and reset them. Six of them had caught gophers. Added to the fifteen from yesterday, that made twenty-one for his first day's trapping. *Not bad. It's not thirty, but it's not bad for my first day. I think I'll get here a little earlier tomorrow and set forty.*

In school that day, Ben applied himself a bit more than he had yesterday. He didn't have time for much homework, now that he was a working man. And he needed his evenings free. He got almost all of his work done in class.

That evening, he finished cutting up the hide.

"Okay," Skeeter said when he had finished, "you see how this long string is all curved and crooked from being cut from a round hide?"

Ben nodded.

"Now gather up the string and come with me."

They walked toward the barn to the water trough by the fence. "Throw it in there."

Wondering, Ben obeyed.

"We'll leave it in there a few minutes," Skeeter explained. "Then we'll hang it up to dry 'til tomorrow. As it hangs, it'll stretch. When it's dry, it'll all be straight."

In a few minutes Ben fished the string out of the water and followed Skeeter into the barn. He helped hang the dripping string from a nail on the wall, looping it across to another nail, back and forth. The heavy wet string sagged between the two nails.

Wednesday's project was to trim both edges of the string so it was all the same width. Skeeter had several cutting gadgets that could be clamped onto the edge of the table. Then they skived the string, shaving it to the same thickness.

The next evening they beveled the edges. By pulling the string along the guide, the blade angled the edge so that it sloped slightly from top to bottom. The string had to be pulled through the cutter twice, once for each side.

By the end of the week Ben began braiding. "Don't we have to grease the strings or something?" he asked as Skeeter showed him how to measure two long strings of equal length.

"The old guys never doped their rawhide,"

Skeeter explained. "They just used a little mutton tallow to grease their riatas or bosals once in a while."

He doubled the two strings, making four strings, and tied one end of the four strands to a nail. They had to be a third longer than the finished seventy-foot riata would be.

"Now leather is different. It's been tanned—rawhide hasn't. It's 'raw.' Before I braid leather, I soak my strings in white gas and glycerine. Here, start your braiding like this." He showed Ben how to make pairs and split pairs. "The gas soaks in and gets that wax into the leather. But never put it on rawhide. It'll make it break down and start curling."

"How did you learn this stuff?" Ben asked with awe in his voice.

"I studied everything I could find. Talked to the old guys that make the real quality stuff."

Studied? Gophers...riatas...I thought once you got out of school, you didn't have to study any more.

Saturday morning Ben got up early. It was much colder. At breakfast, Susie complained about the low temperature. "That freeze wiped out my garden! I guess I'd better bring in what's left of my tomatoes to ripen in the house."

"Might be an early winter," Pete commented, watching the TV weather report as he ate. "We're going to need to get those cows down from the mountain soon."

Ben headed out to do his chores and get to his traps. A thin layer of ice coated the water tank. Breaking it, he watched as Soapsuds thrust his velvety white muzzle into the freezing water. He bobbed his head and snorted as chunks of ice bumped his face.

The ride to Barlows was colder than ever. Dry round tumbleweeds danced across the road in the wind, piling up against the wire fencing. Before running his traps, Ben spent a few minutes rubbing his hands and face to get warm.

It was a disappointing morning. Many traps hadn't been worked, and Ben could hardly find fresh mounds. He had planned to set fifty traps, but he barely found places for fifteen.

Sunday was no better. A stiff north wind howled. Ben only got a few traps set, and most of those didn't catch anything. That night at the bunk-house, he asked Alvin about it.

"What am I doing wrong? I can't seem to catch any gophers this weekend."

Alvin shook his head. "The weather is changing. They don't work when it's real cold."

"The weather report says it's supposed to stay like this for a week or so. Maybe longer," Ben said.

Seth drawled, "Sounds like more bad news for Bad-news Ben."

"Maybe he needs a little Indian summer," said Reggie, winking at Alvin. "Ain't that right, Alvin?"

Alvin smiled his slow smile. "Yeah. A little Indian summer."

"Are they starting to hibernate?" Ben asked.

"Naw, gophers don't hibernate," Alvin said. "They've been packing their nests full of alfalfa roots. That's their winter food supply."

The weather stayed nasty all the next week. Ben faithfully set his traps before school and ran them every afternoon. It didn't take as long now. There were hardly any fresh mounds to set. Besides, John was swathing the field and didn't want any traps underfoot. At least Ben was getting lots of hours in on the riata.

On Friday he turned in his tails, and John paid him for his two weeks of work. He wrote out a check for $235.

Ben's face fell as he took the check. "Thanks," he said half-heartedly. "I didn't catch as many as I hoped. The weather kind of turned bad on me."

"You're a hard worker," John said, "but there's no point in setting any more traps unless the weather improves. Anyhow, I'll be baling and harobedding now—you'd be in the way."

"Oh, I'm sure the weather will improve," Ben replied hastily. "It's got to!"

"Sounds like you needed the money pretty bad."

"Yeah, pretty bad."

The words echoed in Ben's head as he started his four-wheeler and headed home from Barlows, maybe for the last time.

$235 for two weeks looks pretty bad. And part of that goes for gas and to pay Alvin for using his traps. I needed to make $250 each week!

He ducked his head against the bitter wind, shivering hard. *The weather looks pretty bad. My chances of paying for that horse look pretty bad. And the chances of finding more work this time of year look REALLY bad!*

Ben had been hoping to surprise his dad with good news. Now all he had was bad news. Bad-news Ben. He felt like there was a big rock where his heart used to be.

As he rounded the last turn by the barn, he noticed a strange car in front of his house. Pulling into the yard, he saw it was a Cadillac. Brand new. It still had the sticker in the window. Clothes hung on a rack across the back seat. He parked his four-wheeler, jumped off, and raced to the door.

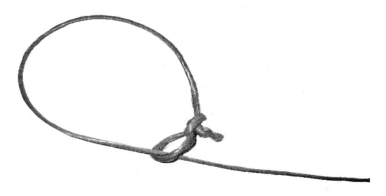

Chapter Ten

Ben burst through the kitchen door and into the living room. A distinguished-looking gentleman and an elegant gray-haired woman, Charles and Francine McFee, put down their coffee cups and rose to greet him.

"There's my little Benjamin! How are you?" his grandmother cooed, hugging him.

"Just fine, Grandma. Hi, Grandpa," he said. Everyone sat down.

"What are you up to, young man?" Mr. McFee asked.

"Oh, not much," Ben answered. "I just got home from work."

"Work?" Mrs. McFee echoed. "And why is a boy your age talking about work? Why aren't you out playing after school?"

Ben glanced at his mother. The look on her face said, "Oh boy, here we go!"

"I heard you drive up on your ATV," Mr. McFee said. "Were you out running around with your friends?" He coughed several times. "Excuse me, I'm just getting over the flu."

"Grandpa, I don't run around with my friends after school. I have things to do," he explained, "and most of my friends do too."

"What kind of things?" Mrs. McFee asked sweetly.

"Work. Like I said," Ben explained. "I have a job after school. Actually I go before school, too, and on weekends. Or at least I did up 'til today."

Mr. McFee's voice now had a bit of an edge to it. "You work before and after school? Doing what?"

"Trapping gophers," Ben said.

"Trapping gophers?" Mrs. McFee repeated, looking shocked. "You kill little animals?"

"Grandma!" Ben laughed. "You trap mice. What's the difference? You kill spiders and flies, too. Everybody does."

"That's different!" she protested. "They are dirty little pests!"

Mr. McFee looked at Susie. "Why do you have this child working before and after school and on weekends?"

"He's not a child, and I don't have him working," Susie said. "It was his idea. His choice. And you know, since he's been working, he gets his homework done without being told."

"Oh, Suzanne Marie," Mrs. McFee said in a disapproving tone. "How could you? Poor little Benjamin."

Ben's eyes flashed, but his voice was polite. "I'm not so little anymore, Grandma. I can do a man's job. And I needed some money."

"My goodness, child, why didn't you just ask your parents?"

"I don't ask my parents for money, Grandma," Ben said. "I earn my own money."

"You know you can ask us whenever you need money," she said with a smile. "We've always told you that."

"And we have always told him not to," Susie interrupted. "Your expensive gifts are enough."

Mr. McFee nodded. "Giving Benjamin nice things is the least that Francine and I can do to make up for the way he's living."

Susie jumped to her feet. "That's enough! Why can't you just accept the way things are and let us live our own lives?" She stomped off to the kitchen and began banging pots and pans around.

Ben didn't know what to do. He looked at his feet.

His grandpa broke the uncomfortable silence. "What do you need money for, Ben?"

Ben hesitated, embarrassed. "I, uh, have to pay the ranch for a horse that died. It was, uh, my fault that he died." *Sheesh! That sounds really stupid after I just said I'm not a kid anymore and can do a man's job. Why did I even bring it up? Too late now.*

"Oh, my. How much do you need?"

"About a thousand dollars," Ben answered.

"Hand me the checkbook, Francine, dear," he said. She dug it out of her purse as he drew his pen from his pocket.

"Stop it, Father!" Susie stood in the doorway, hands on hips. "I heard that little conversation."

"Now, Suzanne Marie, let me help the boy out," her father said. "We can afford it."

"That's not the point," she replied. "Ben, go do your chores and your homework."

Outside, Ben revved his four-wheeler and headed down the dirt road to feed and water the horses. He thought about the scene in the living room. *A thousand dollars. Just like that. Grandpa would give it to me if Mom and Dad would allow it. But they won't.* He sighed.

Ben was finishing his homework when his dad came in. Supper started with the usual small talk. The McFee's told about their latest trip—two weeks in Europe.

Mrs. McFee sighed. "When we went to a piano concert, I just couldn't help thinking, Suzanne Marie, if you had only stayed in California and studied music, you could be performing on a stage like that."

"And if I'd wanted to, I would have," said Susie. "But this is where I want to be. I still play my piano every day. Sometimes I play at church, and I always have a few piano students."

Mr. McFee looked at Pete. "I can find a job for you in my firm anytime you decide to come back to California."

"And how many times do I have to tell you we're not coming back?" asked Pete.

Mrs. McFee didn't seem to know when to quit. "If only Benjamin could have some of the advantages you had as a child," she said to Susie. "And I don't know why you wouldn't let your father give Ben the money."

"What money?" Pete asked suspiciously. Susie filled him in on the conversation before supper.

"Dang it, Charles!" Pete said. "You just can't stop interfering in my family, can you? You and your money!"

"Now Pete, what's wrong with a grandfather wanting to do things for his grandson?" Mr. McFee asked.

"Presents are one thing. Bailing him out of his trouble is another," Pete said. He was quiet a moment, then looked at Ben for a long time, furrowing his eyebrows.

What is he thinking? Ben swallowed hard but held his father's gaze.

"Okay," he finally said. "Ben is not a little kid anymore. He wants to make his own decisions. We'll let him make the call."

He paused. Ben held his breath. "If he wants to take your money, I'll let him. It's up to him. He's got to learn the value of money."

Ben stared at his dad. His eyes widened, and his heart thumped. His dad had just given him permission to take the money! And not only that, his dad had said he wasn't a kid, that he was old enough to make his own decisions. That was almost the same as saying he was a man. He straightened up in his chair, his chest full of pride.

The rest of the meal passed quickly. Ben was busy with his own thoughts. He excused himself from the table. "I'll be right back."

He hurried to the bunkhouse to tell Skeeter he wouldn't be working on the riata that night since he had company.

"And guess what else, Skeeter? My grandpa offered to give me the money I need to pay for the horse. And my dad said it was up to me—I could take it if I want to."

Skeeter said, "Wow!"

Ben looked over at Seth, who raised one eyebrow and said dryly, "Well, it must be nice to have someone that will bail you out whenever you get in a bind."

Ben frowned at Seth's tone of voice as he left. His dad always said he needed to learn the value of money. Well, what better way to show his dad than to pay for that horse? The most important thing was to keep Fred from taking the money out of his dad's check.

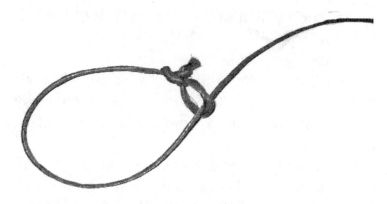

Chapter Eleven

At Saturday morning breakfast, Ben noticed that his grandma wasn't eating anything.

"What's the matter, Grandma? Aren't you hungry?" he asked.

"No, I think I'll just have some tea. I don't feel well."

"I think she's coming down with what I just had," Charles said. "I want to get her home as soon as possible. We'll have to cut our visit short and head on home this morning."

"Oh, darn," Pete said.

Susie shot him a look. "Are you sure you'll be all right, Mother?" she asked anxiously. "Maybe you should stay until you're better."

Ben hoped she'd say yes. He wanted a chance to talk in private to Grandpa about the money.

"No, thank you, dear. We're all packed and ready to leave. Are you done eating, Charles? Let's be on our way."

Charles and Pete shook hands as Francine hugged Susie and Ben. As Charles reached to hug him, Ben hesitated, then stuck out his hand. Charles looked surprised, smiled, and gripped his hand firmly. Ben saw a little grin cross his dad's face.

And just like that, they were gone. *Oh well, I can talk to him on the phone after they get home. At least I can work on the riata all day, since they're gone.*

The next morning, Ben woke up with a stomach ache. He stayed home from church and dragged around the house all day, although he managed to get in some braiding in the afternoon. What little he ate came up in the middle of the night.

On Monday, Ben stayed home from school with a fever. His dad didn't feel well either.

"Isn't this great?" Pete complained to his wife. "Your folks brought us the California Crud." He went to work anyway, as he didn't believe in going to bed when he was sick.

Tuesday found Pete on the couch in the living room. Ben's mother played nursemaid for a couple of days. It was a flu that hit hard and passed quickly. Ben spent a little time braiding while the bunkhouse was empty. He was back in school on Wednesday, and his dad was back at work Thursday.

At supper Thursday night, Pete had some news.

"Fred needs a cleanup crew on the mountain tomorrow and Saturday."

"Cleanup?" Susie asked with a blank look.

"You know—to find the last few stragglers that didn't come down with the main herd last week," Pete explained impatiently.

"Oh, of course," Susie said. Not being from a ranching background, she still had to have things explained to her now and then.

"The problem is, we need three men. But the California Crud has hit the bunkhouse. They're all sicker'n a dirty dog. All except me and Fred."

Ben's head came up. He caught his father's eye. While meeting Ben's gaze, Pete said to Susie, "I'm taking Ben out of school tomorrow. We're going to need him."

"We?" Susie repeated.

Pete gave a short laugh. "Okay, I need him. The heck with Fred. He'll just have to tough it out. Ben's all we've got."

"But can't you just wait until everyone's well?" Susie asked.

"Can't take that chance. The weather report shows a big storm headed our way in a couple of days," Pete explained. "It might very well be the first big winter storm. If we get a big snow, we won't be able to get those cows out. They'll get stranded up there and die."

"Surely you can get one of the hands from another ranch?"

"I could. But I don't want to," Pete retorted. "I want Ben."

"But it's a school day, and he already missed a couple of days this week!"

"He won't miss anything he can't make up, and the things he'll learn this weekend aren't things you can learn in school."

Pete looked at Ben. "What do you say, cowboy? Do you think you can stand old Fred for a couple of days?"

"You bet!" Ben answered, grinning.

After supper, Ben and his dad drove down to the barn. They backed up to a haystack and, with hay hooks, tipped four bales into the bed of the pickup.

"Let's see you back up to the trailer, pardner," Pete said, getting out.

Ben slid over to the driver's side and shifted into reverse. His dad let the tailgate down and stepped back. With his right arm across the back of the seat and his left hand on the wheel, Ben looked over his shoulder, lined up the truck, and backed under the gooseneck until, with a jolt, it caught on the hitch in the middle of the pickup bed. He shut off the motor.

"Atta boy!" Pete said, slamming the tailgate shut. "Couldn't have done better myself."

Ben jumped out and cranked the jack up into place. It felt good to be working with his dad again. Pete took the blocks out from behind the wheels of the trailer, threw them in the truck, and plugged in the brake and light cord. The eighteen-foot stock trailer could hold six horses. It was also used to haul cattle.

Breaking open one bale, they stuffed three hay nets and hung them along the inside of the trailer— one for each pair of horses. Then they drove home, the empty trailer rattling behind them.

The next project was to pack their bedrolls. Cow camp was rather primitive, a tiny one-room cabin with some bunks and a wood-burning stove. At 8,000 feet, night-time temperatures could plunge to well below twenty degrees.

Ben's mom brought out wool blankets and heavy denim quilts she had made from old jeans and lined with red and black checkered flannel. Pete helped Ben spread his canvas tarp on the living room floor and layer it with blankets and his sleeping bag. He showed him how to fold the tarp around it, roll it up and tie it with a length of rope.

"Don't you want a pillow?" Susie asked.

"Naw, we'll just wad up our jackets," Pete said, laying out his tarp.

When they were done, they had two bulky bed-rolls, each about four feet across and two feet high.

"Are you sure you'll be warm enough?" Susie asked anxiously.

"Don't worry," said Pete. "I've stayed warm in a bedroll like this even on the ground in the snow."

"Anyhow, we'll be wearing our long johns, Mom," Ben reminded her.

"What about food?" she asked Pete.

"Fred will take along a few things—bacon, eggs, bread, meat, coffee, canned stuff. And the camp is always stocked with basic supplies."

"How early are we leaving?" Ben asked.

"About three," said his dad. "That'll put us up there ready to ride about five—just before daylight."

"What time should I be up?" Ben asked.

Pete calculated. "We've got six horses to catch, feed, and load up. We've already hooked up the trailer. Two o'clock ought to do it. We'll go to the barn first, then come back here and eat a big breakfast."

Susie moaned. "Oh, you're kidding. Surely you can just get yourselves some corn flakes and toast."

Pete flashed her a stern look. "Hey, if we can be up working at that time of day, I guess you can be up cooking. Anyhow, you can go back to bed after we leave."

"I know, I know," she said, sighing. "You weren't kidding when you warned me about marrying you.

At least I knew ahead of time what kind of life I was agreeing to!" She chuckled. "Oh, what my mother would say about this!"

Pete and Ben laughed too.

This wasn't the first time Ben had got up early to cowboy. But it was the first time his dad had expected him to get up early enough to help with the horses. Just one more sign that his dad thought he was old enough to handle more responsibility.

"Better head for bed, cowboy," Pete said.

Ben glanced at his watch. "Gee, dad, it's only eight."

"I know, but it'll be early soon."

As Ben started for his room, he thought about how strained things had been between him and his dad since the squirrel escapade. He knew his dad was worried about the money and didn't really think Ben would come up with it. He had been hurt by his dad's disappointment in him.

He stopped and turned around. "Hey, Dad?"

"What?" Pete said.

"Thanks."

Pete made a final adjustment on the knot of his bedroll. "Get to bed now, or I'll leave you home!" he said gruffly. But Ben caught the wink his dad gave him. Grinning, he headed for bed.

It was hard to fall asleep this early. Ben squeezed his eyes shut, burrowed into his blankets, and tried to find the most comfortable position. 2 A.M. would arrive all too soon. But he couldn't stop thinking about the next day.

Filling in for one of the cowboys was a man's job. They weren't going to baby him. Would he be able to live up to his father's expectations? Or would he do something stupid again? He wanted his father to be proud of him.

And how about Fred? He had managed to steer clear of Fred since "That Day." Now he'd have to be around him for two whole days. Should he try to be nice to Fred or just avoid him? If Fred lit into him again, what would he do? *Dear God,* he prayed, *please don't let anything go wrong.* Finally he fell asleep.

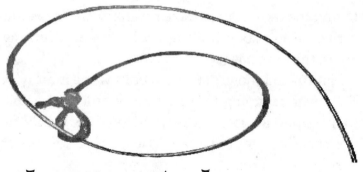

Chapter Twelve

Brrrng! Ben stirred, then leaped to his feet. On a normal day, he let himself wake up gradually before lazing out of bed. But today was different.

He looked at the clock. 2 A.M. There was something about getting up at this hour of day that made you instantly wide awake. Whenever he got up in the middle of the night to go with his dad, it was like this. None of that grogginess that often follows a full night's sleep.

Pete poked his head in the door. "Get up! Morning's half gone!"

Ben pulled on his long john shirt and bottoms, warm socks, jeans, a heavy flannel shirt, and boots. The usual morning smells of coffee and breakfast were strangely absent in the cold house. As he stumbled into the kitchen, he met his mother, bundled in her thick robe, rubbing her eyes and yawning. Pete was already putting on his jacket.

"C'mon, pardner, let's go catch us a couple of cayuses," he said cheerfully.

With the empty gooseneck rattling along behind them, they drove to the barn. The light was on, and Fred was leading a horse into the barn. As Pete and Ben walk in, he turned toward them. His face darkened.

"What's *he* doing here?" Fred growled.

"He's going along," Pete said calmly.

"I thought you said you were going to rustle up someone to help us."

"I did," Pete said.

"I figger'd you meant someone from one of the other ranches."

"Well, I never said that, now did I?"

"What about that Wilson fellow?" Fred grouched. "He's always looking for day work."

"That pencil-neck?" Pete said with a snort. "Having him help would be like losing two good men. He's dead from the butt in both directions."

Pete grabbed a halter and lead rope from a nail on the wall. "Now are we gonna stand here all day jawing, or are we going to get those horses in?"

Fred muttered under his breath. He tied his horse in front of a manger and dumped some grain in it. Ben got a halter and followed his dad out into the dark corral.

The white mare and tall bay gelding stood dozing with the other horses. Pete had brought them up the day before and turned them in with the others, giving all the horses an extra large feeding of hay.

"You catch Whitey," he directed Ben. "You can ride her today and Bones tomorrow."

Ben walked up to the mare and haltered her. Pete caught one of the ranch horses. They took them into the barn, tied them up, and grained them.

With a smirk, Ben caught Bones, the gelding. *No, I won't touch any of Fred's danged old horses.*

Ben, Pete, and Fred each led their extra horse to the trailer. These horses wouldn't be used until tomorrow. It wasn't smart to work a horse hard all day and then work him the next day too. A good cowboy wouldn't use up his horse like that. That's why they each had a string of horses to ride.

Different horses in their string had different abilities. For this weekend, they needed horses that could travel. For other jobs, like sorting pairs, they might want a horse that could cut a cow out of a herd, and for branding or doctoring, one stout enough to handle a big calf or steer on the end of a rope.

Pete led his horse up into the open trailer. The sorrel followed him to the front, where Pete pulled the rope through the bars of the trailer and tied it just long enough so the horse could reach the hay net. Ben loaded his horse next, then Fred loaded his. The horses began munching their hay.

Back in the barn, each of the buckaroos brushed down the horse he'd ride today. They retrieved blankets and saddles from the tack room and threw them onto warm, waiting backs.

"Why can't we just saddle them when we get there?" Ben asked his dad as he stifled a yawn.

"Packing your saddle in the pickup or the trailer is a good way to get it skinned up and bent out of shape." Pete finished buckling the breast collar. "If you'd spent a couple thousand for a good saddle, you'd think about stuff like that. You need to learn the value of money."

Ben glanced over at Fred, who was shaking his head. He vowed not to ask any more stupid questions. In fact, the less he said this weekend, the better. They made one last trip to the tack room for their bridles, chaps, and spurs, which they threw in the back of the truck.

When the three saddled horses were loaded, Pete said, "Well, let's leave these barley-biters to eat their hay while we go get us some grub."

"Suits me," Fred said stiffly. While Ben closed and latched the tailgate, Fred got his bedroll out of his truck and threw it up on the bales in the back of Pete's truck. He drove off toward his house, and Pete and Ben drove home with the loaded trailer.

The warm smells of coffee and bacon beckoned them into the kitchen. Eggs sizzled in hot bacon grease in the skillet. A stack of sourdough hotcakes waited on the table. As Ben slid into his chair, his mother set a steaming mug of fragrant cocoa in front of him. He took a sip and felt the hot liquid trickle down through his chest and into his stomach.

Pete poured himself a cup of coffee and began buttering his hotcakes. With a pot holder, Susie carried the black cast-iron skillet to the table and plopped two quivering fried eggs on top of them. She looked at Ben, who pointed to the side of his plate. She plopped his egg beside his hotcakes and bacon.

"We'll need a couple of lunches, dear," Pete said. "Big ones. Then we'll cook supper at the camp. Get to eating, Ben. I know you're not hungry now, but that breakfast will be feeling pretty good, along about nine-ten o'clock."

Ben sighed and forced down some more hotcakes.

When they could eat no more, they gathered up their gear, putting on warm jackets and their wide-brimmed, high-crowned black felt hats.

"Ben, grab us each a book of matches."

"What for?"

"Always take matches. If you ever get in trouble up there, you can start a sagebrush fire to signal for help and to keep warm."

"Where are you guys headed?" Susie asked.

"Black Ridge camp," Pete said.

He reached for a big, glossy, turquoise scarf that hung on the hat rack. He picked it up by diagonal corners, wrapped it twice around his neck, and tied the ends in a square knot. "You want one of my old wildrags?" he asked, eyeing Ben. "It'll keep your neck warm."

"Nope," Ben said, zipping his jacket. "My collar zips up around my ears."

They hoisted their heavy bedrolls, headed for the pickup, and threw them on top of the hay bales. Susie, shivering in her slippers and robe, followed with their lunches, a small thermos of coffee, and two canteens of water. Pete kissed her goodbye, and they were off.

Ben rolled down his window and hollered, "Hey, Mom, will you do my chores?" She smiled, nodded, and waved goodbye.

Back at the barn, they met Fred.

"Okay then," Pete said. "Let's be off."

Fred whistled. His border collie, Gypsy, jumped out of the back of his pickup and came running.

"Load up," he said. She leaped lightly into the back of the truck and lay down between the bales.

Fred grabbed a box from his pickup and hoisted it into the back of the heavily loaded truck. Pete helped him with a big ice chest.

Oh boy, here we go. Ben climbed into the cab. *Two hours in this truck with Fred. I suppose I'd best just keep my mouth shut. Let them do the talking.*

But nobody talked. The silence was uncomfortable. It was obvious that nobody wanted to be the one to set off sparks.

Ben felt like shrinking down into the seat and disappearing. *This is all my fault. This weekend is going to be one big wreck.*

One little voice in his head said, *Why did I ever agree to come along? I should have stayed home, where I won't cause Dad any more trouble. I'm just a kid, and I always screw things up.*

Another little voice said, *No, I'm not a kid anymore. I'll show them both. No matter how Fred acts, I can take it like a man.*

As the pavement turned to gravel, then dirt, and began to get steeper, Ben drifted off. The warmth of the heater and the roaring of the fan were comforting. The competing voices in his head faded, and then he was asleep.

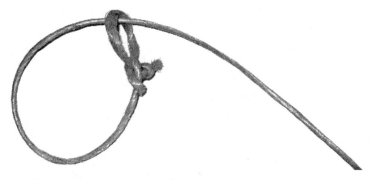

Chapter Thirteen

Ben woke as the pickup rolled to a stop and Pete shut off the motor. The pre-dawn sky hinted at daylight. In the semi-darkness he could make out a little cabin and a set of corrals—Black Ridge camp.

"Well, let's get this outfit unloaded," Pete said.

As Pete and Fred carried the gear inside, Ben unloaded horses. They all needed watering. *I'll even water the ranch horses. We'll just see what Fred has to say about that!*

Ben led the horses, two at a time, to the creek that bubbled from the spring near the cabin. He then tied the saddled horses to the side of the trailer. They snorted and stamped, their frozen breath making little clouds in front of them.

Pete emerged from the cabin and helped Ben finish unloading and watering the horses. With hay hooks, they unloaded the bales of hay and dragged them over by the corral. The three extra mounts were let into the corral and given a generous feeding of hay. Ben wrapped the lunch bags and the thermos in their rain slickers and tied them on the back of his and Pete's saddles. The canteens fit in their jacket pockets.

Ben pulled on his fringed shotgun chaps, buckled the belt, and zipped the legs. He buckled on his short, blunt spurs. He grabbed his bridle from the back of the truck and put it on the old mare. He wanted to be a-horseback before his dad and Fred. That would make a good impression.

Holding the reins and saddle horn, he put his left foot in the stirrup and gave a little hop, pulling himself up. The horn slid toward him as the saddle rolled loosely on the horse's back, and he landed on his rear end.

He had forgotten to tighten the cinch! Fortunately, old Whitey just stood there calmly. *Sheesh! That was about as graceful as a hog on ice.* Still holding the end of the reins, Ben jumped to his feet and pushed the saddle back up into place. He glanced around to see if anyone had noticed his blunder.

Dang! Fred was looking right at him! He shook his head and muttered something under his breath that Ben couldn't make out. *He must think I'm a real gunsel.* He gulped as he realized many horses would have taken that as an excuse to buck. He gave Whitey a grateful pat on the neck. Getting bucked off when you're only halfway in the saddle would not be a good way to start your day.

Furious with himself, Ben straightened the saddle blanket, adjusted the cinch and hoisted himself into the saddle. He couldn't afford any more stupid mistakes. How many times had his dad told him, "Take your time and do it right the first time. The long way is the short way, and the short way is the long way."

Ben knew very well, when you're cowboying, a stupid mistake can cause a wreck or get a man hurt—yourself or someone else. He had to pack his own weight this weekend.

Pete and Fred mounted up, and they all left camp at a high trot, rising slightly up and down in the saddle with every other stride. Gypsy was at their heels. There had been no conversation so far. Nobody told anyone else what to do. That was the buckaroo way. You saw what needed to be done and did it. That's all there was to it.

The crisp morning felt more like winter than fall. Ben pulled his hat down closer to his ears and zipped his jacket all the way, so the collar stood up high. His nose tingled in the frosty air.

It was a long trot to where they'd find the cattle farther up the mountain—maybe two hours' ride.

They'd circle around and gather them all up, then drop them overnight in a trap corral. In the morning, they'd ride back to where they left the cattle and drive them home.

The sure-footed horses made their way easily through the sagebrush—scrubby and low in some places, but tall as a man on horseback where the soil was better. Experienced mountain horses paid attention to where they put their feet, avoiding rocks and badger holes with little direction from their riders. They picked their way through the brush along little trails made by cattle or coyotes.

The Circle A, like other ranches in the area, ran their cattle on these mountains from spring through fall. The mountains were public land— land belonging to the American people but administered by government agencies. The lower sections were administered by the BLM—Bureau of Land Management. The upper regions of the mountains were part of the U.S. Forest Service. Each rancher was assigned a certain area, called an allotment. In this dry barren country, it took a lot of land to run cattle, much more land than most ranchers could afford to buy. Ben wondered if he'd be running cattle on this mountain someday. He rode closer to his dad.

"Hey Dad?"

"Huh?"

"How big of a ranch do you need—to run cattle, I mean?"

"Well, son, that all depends. Depends on how many cattle you want to run. Depends on how good the land is and how much water's available."

"What about here, on our ranch?"

"Well, let's see." Pete was quiet for a moment. "On this place, you've got to figure about fifty acres per animal unit."

"What's that?" asked Ben.

"That's how much ground it takes to support one cow, or one pair—a cow and calf. Now over on Carver's place, they have better land and more water. They're more like thirty acres per animal unit. A guy I went to college with farms on the Washington coast where it rains a lot. Over there it's three acres."

"Gee," Ben exclaimed, "wouldn't it be cheaper to ranch up there?"

"Nope. Land just costs more per acre. And anyhow, there's too much brush...too many trees up there. You can't see anything, like you can out here. Why, he told me he once got lost on his own property. Couldn't see where he was!"

Ben laughed. Not much danger of that in Nevada. Here you could see for miles. Few trees dotted the high desert.

"Dad?"

"Huh?"

"How come you never gave Whitey a real name?"

"Like…Miss Sweetie Pie? Or…Baby Face? I can't see myself calling her that."

Ben laughed.

"She's getting pretty fat," Pete said. "How about…Miss Piggy?"

"Okay, okay, Dad!" Ben laughed. "Just forget it!" He rubbed her neck affectionately.

As they were riding along the barbed wire fence line, they found an open gate—a gate that wasn't supposed to be open. It opened into another rancher's allotment. That meant his cattle could have wandered over into the Circle A herd, or their cattle might have joined up with his.

Fred cussed. "Dang tourists! Why can't they close the gates behind them? It's just common courtesy!"

"Tourists?" Ben said. "Way up here?"

"You know—hunters or backpackers or some such folk. City folk that ain't got no common sense. No wonder our cows are scattered all over heck."

"I'll get it," Ben offered and quickly stepped off his horse.

It was the kind that fastened with a rope. With his reins looped over his arm, he picked up the gate post lying on the ground and set the bottom in the wire loop attached to the bottom of the fence post. After yanking the top of the post to tighten the gate's four strands of barbed wire, he reached for the rope on the fence post.

Instead he slipped and fell on his butt, spooking his horse, who hit the end of the reins and stopped. The post jumped out of the bottom wire and the gate clattered to the ground.

"Get your sorry butt off the ground! Can't you do nothing right?" Fred yelled.

"Aw, for cryin' out loud, Fred," Pete said. "You're makin' my rear end ache."

Ben jumped up and reset the post. Grabbing the rope, he wrapped it twice around the top of the post and reefed on it until the wires were taut. He threw a half hitch over the top, snugged it, and climbed back into the saddle. He stuck out his lip defiantly.

The Circle A, like other ranches, had BLM and Forest Service allotments that it paid to use. It was like renting pasture for their cattle. The different areas were fenced and had water—springs and creeks. Even though the ranchers didn't own the land, they built and maintained fences and watering systems for each pasture.

The allotments were based on the number of cattle they could run. After a time, they moved their cattle from one fenced area to another. This protected the grass from becoming overgrazed. Without good grazing land, they could not make a living from year to year.

Cattle scavenged through the sagebrush for the sparse grass, recycling it into food for humans—beef. Their grazing also controlled the undergrowth that could fuel a lightning fire. Fires were hard to fight in these remote, roadless mountains, and many a rancher had lost much or all of his yearly feed to wildfires.

The allotment system meant that Pete and the other buckaroos spent a lot of time moving cattle. They trailed them up from the winter pastures on the home ranch as soon as the new spring grass carpeted the mountain slopes. Mother cows still nursed calves born a couple of months earlier. The buckaroos branded the new crop of calves, then moved the herd. They scattered salt blocks here and there to entice the cattle to different locations. This prevented overgrazing of any one area.

During the summer, while the cattle grazed up in the mountain pastures, the buckaroos spent much of their time farming, growing hay for winter feeding. They irrigated the alfalfa fields and then cut the alfalfa with a swather—a cross between a tractor and a huge lawn mower.

After drying a few days, the swaths were turned with a huge rotating rake pulled by a tractor. In a few days, when the moisture content was just right, a baler pulled behind a tractor picked up the swaths of cut alfalfa and packed it into bales. Harobeds picked up the bales and stacked them. Working a-horseback every day is a buckaroo's dream, but farming must be done.

Now, in the fall, the mother cows and their half-grown calves had to be brought home before the winter snows trapped them on the mountain. After the fall cattle drive, calves were weaned, sold, and shipped off to California to be fattened on grass before butchering. In winter, the cattle were turned into the dormant hay fields to eat the stubble. When that was gone, they were fed baled hay that had been produced that summer. This was the yearly cycle of ranch life.

By mid-morning the three riders were above the cattle. Fanning out, they pushed the cattle down the mountain. The few cattle that were up there wouldn't be hard to find. As the weather turned colder, they came down to the warmer elevations. During the fall roundup, a week earlier, all the gates in the Circle A allotment had been left open, so the cattle that had been missed could find their way down to lower pastures.

Ben loved riding in the mountains. Quaking aspen and pine trees flourished among tall, round juniper trees. The brilliant gold and orange of the quakies contrasted with the deep green junipers. He loved their Christmas-tree smell and the crunchy sound of the dry pine needles. He reined

Whitey through the trees to spook out a wild-eyed calf. Tail high in the air, it bucked and ran, bawling for its mother.

He spotted a few deer during the day, as well as a group of five bighorn sheep. Whitey took all these sights in stride, but spooked when a pheasant flapped up out of the brush right under her feet. She jumped sideways, but Ben stuck with her. His dad had taught him, "Sit deep in that saddle, no matter how western things get!"

When the sun was quite high in the sky, Ben saw his dad approaching.

"C'mon," Pete called. "Let's shade up by that crick and get out the grub. I'm getting hollow in the flank."

Ben nodded. His stomach was growling, too. He followed his dad to the tree-lined creek. Although there was no snow left from last winter to melt into run-off, springs bubbled up here and there, draining into streams.

Following his dad's example, Ben loosened his horse's cinch and watered her. Then he unhooked his hobbles from where they hung on the back of his saddle. He strapped them in a snug figure-eight around Whitey's front feet and buckled them, then removed her bridle, hung it on his saddle horn and patted her rump.

The hobbled horses grazed freely but couldn't run off or wander too far. Fred joined them, and they unwrapped their lunches. Ben's mom had given him two big sandwiches on her homemade bread—one roast beef and one peanut butter. He wolfed them down and then devoured his apple and chocolate cookies.

"I think I'll have me a little eye-winker," Fred said after he finished eating. He took off his hat and lay down. Pete did the same.

Ben lay down too, but he wasn't very good at napping in the middle of the day, not even in the

warmth of the sun. Watching the grazing horses, he thought about his money problem. He hadn't had any time this week to even think about paying for the horse.

On the days he had been sick, it was the farthest thing from his mind. Back in school, he had so much work to make up, there was no time to think about anything else. And this morning, his thoughts had been occupied with trying not to foul things up. However, the problem hadn't gone away. He thought about the check his grandpa had almost given him and what his dad had said about it.

When I get home, I'll call Grandpa. I'll call him Sunday afternoon, and we'll talk about it. I've got to get the money before Dad's next paycheck. He had no idea how much Fred would take out of it.

Even though Fred had not spoken to him today, his attitude was hostile. Ben had an idea. *Maybe I should tell him today. I'll tell him I can pay for the horse.*

Then he wondered if he should wait until after he talked to his grandpa, or until he actually had the money. *No, Grandpa said I could have it. I know he'll give it to me.*

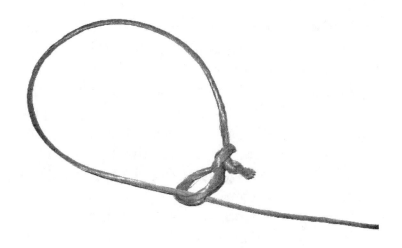

Chapter Fourteen

As Ben rode that afternoon, he tried to decide how and when to tell Fred. Should he catch him alone while they were riding? Should he wait until this evening when they were done working? Should he tell Fred in front of his dad or not? He wondered what Fred would say, and even more important, what his dad would say.

They worked their way back and forth down the mountain, picking up more cows and calves and even a fat, lazy bull. Every time he tried to edge over to where Fred was riding, Fred managed to move away from him. Ben knew that Fred was avoiding him.

Late in the afternoon, Pete rode over. "The trap is just ahead," he said, gesturing. "We'll water these critters, then drop them in there for the night."

The corral had been built near a creek. As the cattle drank their fill, Fred rode on ahead to open the gate. He stationed Gypsy near the gate, where she would head off any animals that tried to break out of the herd. Slowly the three riders pushed the cattle toward the gate.

Pete and Fred worked the sides, and Ben pushed them from the rear. Once the leader went in, it wasn't hard to keep the rest of the cows following her.

A wily, black cow rolled her eyes at Ben and tried to run back past him. Legging Whitey, he was instantly head to head with her. She slung her horns wickedly and tried to hook him. Whitey, an old experienced cow horse, anticipated and blocked her every move. The cow soon gave up and fell back into line.

Ben glanced over to see if Fred had noticed how he handled that cow. But Fred's sunglasses made it hard to tell which way he was looking.

As the last stragglers plodded through the gate, Gypsy nipped at their heels to hurry them along. Fred shut the gate.

"Well, that didn't go too badly. Look, they're already starting to mother up," Pete said.

Cows and their calves, separated along the way, bawled as they found each other in the herd. Others settled down and began to graze on the sparse dry grass growing in the large enclosure.

"We've got a long trot home. Let's get going, Ben."

Fred had already struck out for camp ahead of them, with Gypsy loping easily at his side.

That's okay. Probably the best time would be after they had finished dinner and were sitting around the cabin, relaxing. The truth was, he didn't want to talk to Fred. The longer he could put it off, the better.

Except...the longer he put it off, the more anxious he felt. There were those doggoned little voices in his head again, telling him different things. *Tell him now...No, wait just a little longer.* It was hard to know which one to listen to.

Back at camp, they tied the tired, sweaty horses to the trailer. Pete and Fred went inside to light a fire in the stove, start dinner, and get some buckets for hauling water.

Ben unsaddled and brushed down the horses. He hung the saddles over the sides of the pickup bed and turned the wet saddle blankets upside down on top of them. Picking up each of the horses' feet, he checked for rocks. With a lead rope in each hand, Ben headed for the willow-lined creek to let two of the horses drink. He hung the ropes over his elbow while he stooped over to scoop up clear, icy water in his hands.

Before he could bring it to his mouth, a crashing sound in the brush startled the horses. Ben's head jerked up as two deer leaped out of the willows and bounded away. He grabbed for ropes as the horses jumped. One landed on Ben's foot.

"Ow!"

The other spun around behind Ben and pulled back, jerking the rope across Ben's neck.

"Whoa...whoa there," he crooned, reeling in his lead ropes. The snorting horses settled down and returned to their drinking. After putting them away, he watered the third horse and the ones in the corral.

Ben turned all the horses loose in the corral and threw them a generous feeding of hay. Limping on his bruised foot, he headed for the cabin. His nose crinkled and his mouth watered as he caught the aroma of fried steak and boiled coffee. Eagerly following his nose, he limped faster. His dad approached from the spring with two buckets of water.

He'd say nothing to his dad about his foot or neck. Ben wouldn't complain or look for sympathy—that was not the cowboy way. His dad would just say, "Tough it out! Act like a man!" *Well, I'm tough. I'll show him I'm tough.*

Fred was turning the fried potatoes in a big, black, cast-iron skillet. Three steaks sizzled in another huge skillet. A kettle of water for washing up after dinner simmered on the back of the wood-burning stove.

"Can I help?" Ben asked. He didn't really want to help Fred, but he wanted to make a good impression.

Fred stared at him, taking in his limp. "NOW what did you do?" he asked with sarcasm.

"It's nothing," Ben said.

"What's that on your neck?" Fred demanded accusingly.

"Just a little rope burn," Ben said. "They spooked at a couple of deer while they were drinking."

Fred snorted and tossed his head. "It's a miracle you didn't let them get away!"

"I didn't do anything wrong!" Ben said. "All they did was just jump around a little!" *So much for making a good impression.*

He limped over to the table, picked up the can opener and opened the green beans and peaches that Fred set out. Pete was staring at him with his lips set tight.

Ben shrugged his shoulders, then set out bread, butter and jam. When dinner was ready, they sat down and heaped their plates.

As Ben ate, his chest tightened. He knew he had to say something soon. He hated to start a confrontation with Fred. A knot formed in his stomach, and his head started throbbing.

Suddenly, he was just dog-tired all over. As the long day caught up with him, he could hardly hold his head up to finish eating. He stumbled to his feet and stacked his dirty dishes, mumbling something about dishwater.

Pete chuckled. "I think you'd best just hit the sack. You've got another long ride ahead of you tomorrow, pard."

Yawning, Ben nodded, kicked off his boots, stripped down to his long johns, and crawled into his bedroll. The moment he stretched out his aching body, he was dead to the world.

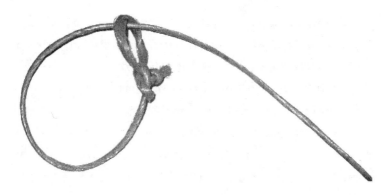

Chapter Fifteen

The next thing Ben knew, his dad was shaking him by the shoulder. "Ben! On your hind legs!"

Ben rolled over and rubbed his eyes. "What time is it?" he mumbled.

"Four o'clock."

With a jolt he was wide awake. Sitting up on the edge of his bunk, he rubbed his eyes and ran his hands through his hair. The rope burn on his neck stung.

"C'mon, let's go see to the horses while Fred starts breakfast," Pete said, grabbing his jacket.

Ben yawned and pulled on his clothes and boots. Wincing, he stifled a groan. The rope burn on his neck chafed under his collar. He quickly found some bag balm in his dad's first aid kit and dabbed the soothing ointment on the burn.

When they returned from feeding and watering the horses, Fred was heaping a plate with crisp bacon. He dropped eggs into the sizzling fat in the big skillet. In another skillet he had heated up the leftover spuds from last night's dinner.

Holding slices of bread over the flame with a pair of tongs, Fred made a few pieces of toast. There was just time before breakfast to roll up their bedrolls and make some sandwiches for lunch.

Pete poured coffee into three tin cups and handed one to Ben.

"Here, this'll warm your innards."

There was no milk or sugar to doctor it with. Ben sipped the strong brew and shuddered at its bitterness.

Fred seemed more cantankerous than usual this morning, if that was possible. He banged around, cussing and muttering to himself.

Slamming the clean tin plates on the table, he bellowed, "Come and get it!" but his tone of voice was not at all inviting.

Unlike yesterday, Ben's dad didn't have to nag him about eating. Today he ate a humongous breakfast, sopping up canned tomatoes with his spuds and toast. He finished his coffee, all but the last few swallows, which were full of grounds. Getting up, he hoisted the water kettle from the back burner of the stove and started to pour hot water into the dishpan.

"I'll do dishes this time."

Fred leaped to his feet and grabbed the kettle away from Ben.

"Leave it be! I don't need no help from you!" he bellowed.

"Fine!" Ben said, backing away and throwing his hands in the air like a crook that's been caught in the act. He added, "What's your problem today, anyway?"

"You!" Fred bellowed. "I don't need no dang kid helping me in the kitchen. And I sure don't need you helping me with my dang cows!"

Ben looked helplessly at his dad.

Pete made an impatient face. "Fred's on the hook this morning," he said.

Ben almost laughed at the mental picture of Fred slinging his horns around. He asked, "What are we doing today?"

"We're going to ride down to the trap where we left the cows, take them farther down the mountain. Then Fred will ride back up here about noon, break camp, load the extra horses, and drive home. You and me'll take the cows the rest of the way down."

Fred exploded. "He can't even saddle a horse right!" He sloshed the dishwater. "How's he going to drive my cows? That useless, sorry excuse for a hand!" He glared at Pete. "Why didn't you get me a real hand, someone I could depend on?"

"For crying out loud!" Ben said in exasperation. "You can depend on me."

"For what?" Fred thundered. "To get another one of my horses killed?"

"Hey, now, that's enough of that," Pete snapped. "You lay off him! I'll have you know that my boy is planning to pay for that horse out of his own money. He's earning it all himself, and I'm dang proud of him for doing it."

That little speech set Ben back on his heels. He didn't know what to say. His dad was sticking up for him against Fred! On the other hand, his dad's announcement just wrecked his plan.

But there was no time to think. Fred and Pete were arguing. Something about how Pete had better watch it. Ben snapped back to attention.

"Cripes, he's just a kid!" Pete said.

"Well, I didn't hire your kid, now did I?" Fred snarled. "And I'm beginning to be sorry I ever hired *you*."

"Oh, so that's what it's coming down to!" Pete's voice rose and his face turned red. "Well, maybe you can just take your job and shove it."

Ben gasped, horrified at what he heard. He knew his dad had a temper, but he had never known him to lose it at work.

"Fine, then! When you and Wonder Boy get those cows down off the mountain—IF you ever do—maybe you better just pack it up and start looking for a new place to spread your bedroll."

Ben felt like someone had just punched him in the belly. His dad stared at Fred.

"C'mon, Ben," he said in a voice that chilled Ben. "Let's get out of here."

Ben grabbed his jacket and followed. As he went out the door, he shot Fred a black look, muttering under his breath, "I hate you!" He slammed the door behind him.

In a silent fury, Pete stalked toward the corral. Ben hurried to catch up. He caught his dad's tall bay gelding.

"Come on, Bones," he said, leading him out through the gate behind Pete and his horse. The other horses tried to follow, but Ben only let Bones through. He remembered the time he hadn't been quick enough, and a horse got out. That was when he was young and irresponsible. *None of those kinds of mistakes today.* He had learned from his mistakes.

After tying Bones to the gooseneck, he brushed him, running his other hand along behind the brush. He loved the look, the feel, and the smell of a horse. The soft snuffing of his breath, his big warm brown eyes, and his sleek muscular contours soothed the shaky feeling in Ben's middle.

He laid the blankets in place, folds to the front, over the horse's high bony withers. Holding his heavy saddle by the front and back, he hoisted it high as he swung it up and over, letting it fall into place.

He soon had the horse cinched up and bridled and had buckled on his chaps and spurs. He circled Bones once to let the air out of his belly, then remembered to tighten the cinch before getting on.

Bones was tall, a good sixteen hands. The reins in his left hand, Ben stood next to Bones' shoulder and grabbed a hunk of mane. With his right hand, he turned the stirrup toward him; he barely managed to reach it with the toe of his left boot.

Bouncing on his right foot, he reached for the horn with his right hand. He jumped and heaved himself into the saddle, pulling back on the reins, for Bones had started forward during all that hopping around.

"Whoa," Ben said as he adjusted his reins and found the stirrup with his right foot.

Pete rode up beside him, his mouth tight and his eyes hard. Ben wanted to ask him questions, but dared not. Not when his dad was in this kind of mood.

Looking at Ben, Pete nodded his head to the side, and they moved out together. Fred had not yet appeared.

They trotted off in the dim light. The air was thin, cold, and crisp. Unlike yesterday on old, fat Whitey, Ben had no trouble keeping up with his dad. Bones was fresh and eager to go. A big rangy Thoroughbred type, he was built to travel.

As the horses settled into a rhythmic gait, Ben's thoughts returned to the scene in the kitchen. *Dad said I could decide for myself about the money, but I don't think he really wants me to take it. Now he says he's proud that I'm earning it all myself! What would he think if I got it from Grandpa?*

Ben wanted so much for his dad to be proud of him. And his dad had actually said the words--said them to Fred! *I can't let Dad down now. I can see the look I'd get if I mentioned Grandpa. What should I do?* He fretted as he rode.

Finally they reached the trap. The cattle were going to want to head for water as soon as the gate was opened. But this morning they would not be allowed to drink. With their bellies full of water, they'd be slow and hard to drive. Cattle tend to want to go back to the last place they watered, but now they needed to head for home on the flats where they could drink their fill. Thirsty cattle will line out and travel, because they think they're being taken to water.

Pete and Ben stationed themselves between the gate and the creek.

"Where's Fred?" Ben asked, looking around.

"Dang if I know. Guess he's having himself a bit of a hissy fit," said Pete. "We'll play heck to keep these old blisters out of the crick, just you and me."

As Pete rode over to the gate, he took down his lass rope, shook it out, and built a big loop. "Get ready—things are gonna get a little western. Here they come!"

He reached over and unlatched the gate. As it swung open, he turned his horse back toward the creek. Out they came.

Ben and Pete charged their horses toward the leaders, shouting, "Haaa! Haaa! Hey-yah!"

The first cow made a dash past Ben. He clapped Bones smartly with his stirrups. In two long, graceful strides, Bones was in front of her. She slung her head, bawled, and did an about-face.

Right behind her came a big calf. Ben turned Bones sharply to the left. Bones pivoted on his hind foot. His powerful hind legs dug in as he lunged at the calf, ears back, head down, right in its face.

"Haaa! Git!"

The first cow had circled back, and Pete tried to cut her off. More cows crowded him, milling and bawling. Pete swung his rope hard in their faces, the huge loop hissing and whistling like something alive. He let them feel the bite of it as it stung them like a monstrous hornet.

Ben spied Fred racing toward them at a dead run. He rode between the herd and the water, Gypsy right behind him. She nipped at heels and leaped in faces, fearless before the bawling bovines.

Now they began to make some headway. Pete got a few started away from the water, returning to help turn some more to follow the leaders. Fred and Ben stayed by the creek, working back and forth, their skillful horses making agile turns and quick dashes.

One old cow wasn't going to give up, though. Slinging her horns, she just kept coming with a menacing look in her eyes. Fred whistled.

Instantly Gypsy was in her face. She leaped, grabbing a mouthful of ear. Hanging on, she dangled above the ground.

Furious, the old cow bawled and slung her head. She couldn't shake the dog loose from her ear.

Her resolve began to weaken. Gypsy hung on, the whites of her eyeballs showing as she rolled her eyes toward Fred, waiting for further direction. The old cow began to circle away from the water, her head hanging lower and lower, dragging the dog.

"Gypsy. That'll do!" Fred said in a business-like tone. She let go, fell, and scrambled to her feet.

"Cranky old sow! Guess that'll soften her up," Fred said. He made one last charge at her with his horse, and off she trotted with the rest of the herd.

"Wow!" Ben said, laughing. For a moment he forgot his feud with Fred. "How did you teach her to do that?"

"I didn't. She just does it," Fred said. "She won't quit unless I tell her."

Fred and Ben moved off after the cattle. Looking for any remaining strays, the riders began moving the small herd down the mountain. As they rode, they picked up a few more cows and calves that were clustered in heavier grazing areas.

Several carried a brand other than the Circle A. Ben recalled the open gate. When they got back home, these would have to be sorted out of the herd.

The wind tugged hard at Ben's hat, and he noticed uneasily that cloud banks had moved in. Not the towering white thunderheads of summer, but the bleak gray shapeless snow clouds of winter.

Dad was right. We've got to get these cattle home before it snows.

By mid-morning, all the cattle were accounted for. It was now merely a matter of opening the gates between here and home and making sure no stragglers got separated from the herd. Ben rode drag, keeping the slowpokes moving along. Every so often one tried to quit the herd, and it was Ben's job to change its mind.

Fred, being cow boss, rode at the head of the line of cattle, keeping them pointed in the right direction.

The ones in front wanted to go much faster than the stragglers in the rear. Every time they came to a gate, Fred held up the leaders until the rest of the herd caught up. Otherwise they'd have a line of cattle stretched much too far for three men to handle.

Pete rode over to join Fred, and Ben reined Bones in their direction. As he pulled up, Pete stepped off his horse and untied his slicker from the back of his saddle, pulling out his thermos.

Pouring himself a cup of coffee, he said stiffly to Fred, "I guess we can take it from here. You headed back to camp now?"

Fred leaned on his wide flat saddle horn. His mouth tightened. He looked over at Ben.

"I told that boy I don't want him under foot! At least I've been here to keep an eye on him up 'til now. I don't like him riding herd on my cattle when I'm not around!"

Oh no, here we go again.

Pete rolled his eyes. "You know we've got us a bunch of sick cowboys at home. We've got to get the job done with what we have."

"You could've hired someone to help us for a couple days!"

"I got someone to help. And he ain't costing you nothing."

"I don't want him around my cattle when I ain't here! I don't trust him!"

Trying to control his mouth, Pete bit his lip and looked away. He sipped his coffee.

"Okay. Here's the deal," he said evenly. "Ben doesn't go with the herd. He goes home with you. I'll manage alone." He stared at Fred, daring him to argue. "All I've got to do is open gates, ride along behind these old girls and peck on their butts. They know the way."

Ben felt like he'd been body-slammed. *No, no, no! How can Dad do this to me?* He didn't want to go with old Fred. He wanted to ride with his dad.

Fred's eyes narrowed, and he stared at Pete.

"Go on," Pete said. "You take him with you."

Fred gave Ben a look that would wilt a fence post. It was obvious that he didn't want to take Ben, but there was nothing he could say. There was no other option. He jerked his horse around, rudely kicking him into a lope.

"Aw, Dad," Ben pleaded.

"Just go." Pete's voice was stern. There would be no arguing with him. "Don't give him any guff. Just do whatever he says, and if there's any trouble, I'll deal with it when we get back."

With a heavy heart, Ben reined his horse around and followed Fred, making no effort to catch up.

As they neared camp, Bones began snorting and spooking. Ben tried to figure out what had Bones on edge. Finally he spotted some mountain lion tracks.

Ben was no tracker, but he could see they were fresh. Bones blew hard and shook his head at the wild scent as he crossed the tracks. He minced his steps and arched his neck.

Again and again the tracks appeared. Ben thought of his dad's guns back at camp in the pick-up. The gun rack in the back window held a .22 and a .30-30. The .22 wouldn't be much force against a mountain lion. He was glad he also knew how to use the bigger rifle, the lever-action .30-30.

I wish I had it with me. Oh well, it's nothing to worry about. Mountain lions were common up here, but he had never seen one.

Fred continued to stay well in front. Ben and Pete had stuffed some sandwiches into their pockets before they left, and Ben ate his as he rode. That way he'd be free to help Fred as soon as they got to camp.

He tied Bones to the trailer alongside Fred's horse. Gruffly, Fred pointed toward the cabin. "Throw the food and the bedrolls in the truck. Then come out and help me."

"Want me to fix you a sandwich?" Ben offered.

"Ain't hungry," Fred snapped.

Sorry I asked, said Ben sarcastically to himself.

In the cabin, Ben saw that Fred had neatly boxed

up the supplies. First he carried the box to the pick-up, then dragged the ice chest, which was much lighter than it was yesterday. That left the bedrolls, which they had each rolled up and tied when they got up. He loaded Pete's heavy bedroll, then Fred's.

As he hauled his own bedroll through the cabin door, a blood-curdling scream, like the scream of a woman, cut through the air. Dropping the bedroll, Ben saw a half-grown mountain lion on the far side of the corral.

Fred, in the corral with only the sorrel left to catch, looked around. Gypsy raced toward the cougar, and at the same moment, the panic-struck sorrel bucked and squealed. A hoof struck Fred on the side of the head. He crumpled and fell.

Ben heard vicious snarling as Gypsy tangled with the big cat. Gypsy howled pitifully, then there was silence. The cat streaked away.

Horrified, Ben ran toward the corral. "Fred! Fred!"

There was no answer. Fred didn't move.

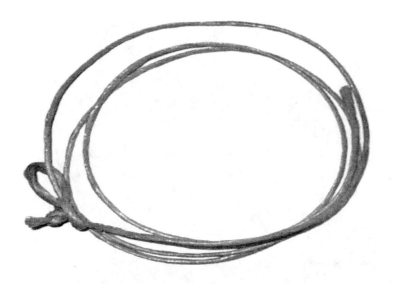

Chapter Sixteen

The two saddled horses tied to the trailer snorted, pulling back on their ropes and dancing around. A clattering of hooves came from inside the trailer, where Fred had already tied two of the horses from the corral.

Ben ignored them as he ran by. Crawling between the rails, he hurried to Fred's still form.

"Fred! Are you okay?"

No answer. A pool of blood formed slowly under Fred's head.

Ben's heart was pounding. He looked around at the snorting sorrel gelding. He was still racing

around, twisting and bucking. Ben stayed between him and Fred.

Ben grabbed Fred under his arms and pulled him toward the fence, keeping his eye on the horse. The gaunt old man was surprisingly light. *He can't weigh as much as me.* His boot heels dragged in the dirt, making two parallel lines.

At the fence, Ben laid him down, crawled through, then reached under to pull Fred the rest of the way to safety. He gently let him down.

Shaking all over, he fought against panic. He thought of his dad, too far away to help. *I wish I knew first aid. Come on!* he scolded himself. *Use common sense!*

Bending over Fred's chest, he listened for a heartbeat. *Good.* The chest moved up and down. He sighed with relief. *Okay, we're still in business. Now, about that bleeding.*

He looked around, thinking. A whimper from the other side of the corral distracted him. *Gypsy! Oh, poor Gypsy.*

Then he had another thought. *The cougar—what if it comes back?*

He ran to the pickup, got the .30-30 out of the rack above the seat, found the ammunition in the glove compartment, and loaded the gun. He raced back to Fred's side, laid the gun down, and felt in Fred's back pocket. Sure enough, he found a handkerchief.

"I hope this is clean enough," he muttered.

Ben gently picked up Fred's head and forced himself to examine the ugly wound. The blood was all over the side of his head, but the cut was just above his left ear. Fred's skull showed where the skin was peeled back.

Ben looked away, swallowing hard. He'd seen hurt animals before, but never a person. "Tough it out! Cowboy up!" his dad always said. *I've got to stop that bleeding!*

He took a deep shuddering breath. Gingerly, he pressed the folded handkerchief against the wound. Reaching into his jacket pocket, he pulled out the long, orange twine he had stuffed in there weeks ago. One end was still tied in a slipknot.

He wrapped it around Fred's head several times, snugly securing the bandage. He knotted it as tightly as he could. *Okay. Now what?*

Another wave of panic swept over Ben as he realized how grave the situation was. He had to get Fred out of here—now.

He looked around the camp. The wind pierced his clothes like sharp needles of ice. Murky clouds swallowed up the mountain, and tiny snowflakes drifted past Ben's face.

"Oh great," he said out loud. "That's all I need."

He thought of leaving the horses and trailer here and just taking the truck, but chucked that idea. *If it bogs down and snows, the horses will be stranded. I'm not about to be responsible for letting five more horses die. No, I've got to take them with us. And if worst comes to worst, I can always use one to ride out.* He heaved a deep sigh.

Taking the gun, he returned to his bedroll. He was only dimly aware of his sore foot and hardly bothered to limp at all. Untying the bedroll, Ben pulled out the denim quilt, carried it to the pickup, and spread it out on the seat. He threw the rest of the bedroll in the back, not bothering to roll it up. He set the ice chest on it so it wouldn't blow out.

Ben tried to pick Fred up. Fred moved. His eyelids fluttered, then opened for a moment. Seeing Ben, he smiled a wobbly smile.

"Joey!" he said in a weak voice. He drifted off again.

"Fred!" Ben said anxiously. "Fred, wake up! We've got to get you to the pickup."

He slung Fred's arm around his neck and hoisted him to his feet. Fred came to again, staggering drunkenly as Ben pulled him along. He shoved Fred into the passenger side, wrapped the quilt around him, and shut the door.

Ben loaded Bones and Fred's horse, leaving their saddles on. Still no cat. He grabbed his gun anyway, carried it to the corral, and propped it within easy reach.

The sorrel had calmed down, and Ben easily caught and loaded him. He slammed the tailgate shut and secured it. With a deep breath, he looked around. Seeing Fred's hat, he grabbed it and threw it in the cab of the truck.

He hurried to retrieve the gun leaning against the fence, only to hear Gypsy's pitiful whine again. Ben groaned. Gun in hand, he found her on the other side of the corral.

"Oh, Gypsy!" he whispered, tears coursing down his cheeks. He dropped to his knees and tenderly touched her shoulder. One side of her face was shredded from her ear to her lips. Guts spilled from her badly ripped belly. She had lost a lot of blood.

Maybe I should try to get her to a vet. But he doubted even a vet could repair this mess. Besides, Fred was his first priority. He got up slowly and picked up the gun. Heartbroken, he walked away.

She whimpered again.

Ben stopped. After a long pause, he turned around. He wanted to throw up. He cranked the lever down, then back up, and wiped his eyes. He shouldered the gun and sighted down the barrel. He hesitated. His whole body trembled. With a deep breath, he steadied the heavy rifle and squeezed the trigger.

"Boom!"

Everything went quiet. Ben stood still, lowering the gun and shuddering. A sob escaped from his violently shaking body. The only sound now was the vicious howling of the wind and the stamping of horses' feet in the trailer.

Sniffling hard, he wiped his eyes again, then remembered Fred. There was no time to lose. No time for feeling sorry. His legs felt wooden, but he forced himself to run back to the pickup.

Everything was loaded. Time to go.

After emptying the gun and putting it in the rack, he started the motor. One glance at Fred's grayish-white, blood-streaked face told him he was unconscious again.

Ben stuffed more quilt between the door and Fred's head for padding. He shifted into low gear and eased out of the yard.

The heavy trailer behind the pickup felt strange to Ben. He was suddenly thankful for his driving experience, but he'd never pulled a loaded trailer. He had never driven in the mountains. And he didn't like the looks of the weather one bit.

"Oh God, please help me, please," Ben prayed under his breath.

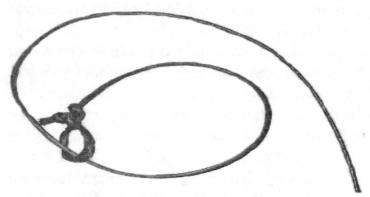

Chapter Seventeen

I wish I hadn't been asleep on the way up here, Ben thought as he pulled out of the camp. *If I'd been awake, I'd have a better idea of what to expect on this road. Oh well. Here goes.*

He tried to remember the past trips he'd made up here with his dad in other years. Two words came to mind: steep and bumpy.

The tires slid to the left on the big rounded rocks, then to the right. The trailer lurched slowly along behind. Iron-shod hooves clattered as horses struggled to keep their balance.

Fred stirred, groaning. Ben brought the rig to a smooth halt.

"Fred? You okay?...Fred?"

Fred's eyes opened. Seeing Ben, he gave a bleary smile. "Joey! Joey!"

Ben frowned. *Fred must be delirious, but he seems to be coming around.* Letting his foot off the clutch, he started up again. Just ahead, the road began to rise steeply. He gunned it toward the top of the hill. The engine whined. *I should have taken a run at the hill farther back. I've got to plan ahead.* His adrenaline was pumping as he reached the crest and the road straightened out briefly. He sighed with relief.

Snowflakes dotted the windshield now. The heater finally warmed up and blasted hot air. The roaring fan only worked on high. He reached over and felt Fred's forehead. Cool and clammy. Fred was out again.

I don't believe this. This is the worst day of my whole life.

The scene at camp played over and over in his mind. He kept hearing the cat's scream, seeing Fred fall, and hearing Gypsy's sad cry. Tears came to his eyes, partly for what had happened, but partly because he felt sorry for himself.

"Why did this have to happen to me?" he said out loud in an anguished voice. "Why couldn't Dad have been there? Why did you let this happen, God? I prayed that nothing would go wrong!"

He had a hopeful thought—maybe he'd meet his dad and the cattle going down the hill! He looked around. It didn't hurt to keep an eye out.

I never did talk to Fred about that money. I'll do that

as soon as he's okay. He looked at Fred and thought, *please be okay.* What if he wasn't okay?

The snow was thicker, the flakes big as quarters. Ben turned on the wipers. His thoughts returned to the money and that argument this morning between his dad and Fred. Could it really have been only this morning? It seemed so long ago.

Ben realized with a sickening feeling that he couldn't ask his grandpa for the money like he had planned. Not now. Not after what his dad had said. He finally let himself admit the bothersome thought that had been in the back of his mind all this time. Why should his grandpa pay for Ben's mistake? It was the easiest way out, but it just wasn't right.

Ben remembered what he'd told Seth in the barn the day of the squirrel fiasco. "A man's got to take responsibility for his actions." Now he realized that he had known it all along but hadn't wanted to admit it. It would be so easy to accept his grandpa's offer, but in his heart of hearts, Ben cared deeply about what his dad thought of him.

The wet snow blurred the windshield. Rounding a turn, the truck slid just a little. Ben's heart skipped a beat as he steadied the wheel and straightened out his rig.

"I think I'd better put her in four-wheel drive," he said out loud, trying to calm himself.

Stopping, he got out and turned the hubs on the front wheels. Back in the cab, he shifted into 4WD, let out the clutch smoothly, and started off in low gear. The road evened out for a ways, and Ben relaxed his death grip on the steering wheel. His jumbled thoughts drifted as he drove.

A thousand dollars. I need a thousand dollars. And I need it quick.

He thought about selling his four-wheeler. No, that was a gift. The computer? That was a gift too. And even if he did sell them, his grandparents would just give him another one. His dad would say it was no different than asking them for the money.

Ben thought hard. What else did he have of value? Something worth as much as a horse?

A horse. Of course. Soapsuds.

Panic gripped Ben's heart. *No. Not my colt!* Then that other voice: *Yes. The colt. There's nothing else left. And Dad's really hurting for money now, since he's quitting, or getting fired, or something. I've got to help Dad.*

Ben knew Soapsuds must be worth $1,000. His dad said he had good conformation: straight legs, high withers, a good slope to his shoulders, a long hip, and a kind, intelligent eye. He wasn't broke yet, but he'd make a good ranch horse.

How could I part with him? My most prized possession...

He looked at Fred. *Just because of that grouchy old man,* he thought angrily.

Well, that wasn't entirely true, he admitted to himself. It was because of his own irresponsibility. Now he must pay the price. His dad always said, "You reap what you sow."

Suddenly the road changed dramatically. The scene ahead jerked Ben from his thoughts. He stopped and looked things over.

They had reached the summit. As the wind blew aside a curtain of snow, he saw a small plane flying below them over the valley. He could just make out their ranch. From his vantage point it seemed as small as a postage stamp. Then it disappeared in murky gray.

Looking over at Fred, Ben worried about how long it was taking to get him to the hospital. This road was slow under the best conditions. The weather and his driving ability didn't help.

What if I slide off the road? Ben shuddered. He'd have to go real slow. *Better to get to the doctor late than never.*

He shifted into the lowest gear. Ben's biggest fear was sliding off the road. But if he rode his brakes too hard, they might heat up. He knew he could lose them on this long hill. He remembered his dad mentioning the bad switchbacks.

Taking a deep breath to calm himself, Ben let his

foot off the clutch. The truck growled and crawled slowly forward. The windshield wipers beat a steady rhythm like the metronome on his mother's piano.

Ben had no idea how badly Fred was hurt. What if he died before Ben could get him to town? Because of Ben, a horse had died. Then he had to shoot poor, sweet, old Gypsy. Now, if Fred died, it would be his fault. Nausea clutched at his stomach again.

This is the absolute worst day of my life. I hate this place—these mountains. I used to think they were beautiful, friendly—the guardians of our valley. But they're not. They're cold and cruel.

Ben gripped the wheel tighter as he reached the first hairpin turn to the right. He got as far to the left edge of the road as he could, riding his brakes. Then he cramped the wheel hard to the right, hugging the inside of the turn. He let out his breath.

"Made it," he said aloud. "Thanks, God!" Adrenaline pumping, he took a deep breath, then straightened out the truck.

Why did my dad ever want to live in a place like this? Grandma's right. It's so...uncivilized. As soon as I'm old enough, I'm out of here.

"Huh? What's going on?" Fred mumbled as he came to again. He reached for his head, then looked over at Ben. "What are you doing?" he asked.

"I'm taking you to the doctor," Ben said.

Relief washed over him like a warm shower. "I thought maybe you were going to die on me."

"Don't hold your dang breath," Fred said slowly and painfully. "Anyhow, I thought you said you hated me."

Ben's face turned flaming hot. He hadn't meant Fred to hear that.

"Not enough to let you die," he answered.

He brought the pickup to a stop and shifted into neutral. "Boy, am I glad you woke up. Here, you want to drive?"

Fred looked around, confused. "Where are we, anyhow?... Oh cripes! How'd you get here?"

"Very slowly," Ben said. "The road's pretty bad. I think you'd better drive."

Fred turned to look out the back, clutching his head and groaning. "You got all the horses?"

Ben nodded.

"Where's my hat?"

Ben pointed. He looked at Fred curiously. "Do you remember what happened?"

"Kind of," Fred said. "I heard a cat scream."

"You got kicked in the head. How do you feel?"

Fred touched the wound and flinched. "Not too shiny. Like I been hit by a truck. Where's Gypsy?" he asked, looking out the back window again.

Ben looked down. "The cougar got her. She's... I had to..." He couldn't finish. Sniffing, he wiped tears from his cheeks.

Fred groaned. Rubbing his eyes, he said, "I'm seeing double."

"But...can't you drive?" Ben asked anxiously.

Fred chewed his lip and peered out the window.

"I don't think so, boy," he said in a quiet voice. "You got us this far. You better just keep on going."

Ben took a deep breath and let it out slowly. Reaching for the gearshift, he got the truck rolling again. The road was muddier now, and he was conscious of Fred's critical eye.

The next switchback twisted to the left. Approaching the turn, he again pulled as far as he dared to the outside edge. Then he cranked it hard to the left, riding his brake. Between the rocks and the mud, he didn't have much traction, and he felt the trailer sliding toward the edge with the steep drop-off.

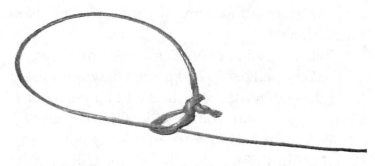

Chapter Eighteen

"Whoa, there!" Fred called, peering out his window. With a pounding heart, Ben clutched the wheel and braked to a halt.

Fred's eyes never left his side window. Ben could see he was looking straight down the drop-off.

"How close am I?" Ben asked, his voice shaky.

"You don't really want to know."

They started up again. "You sure you don't want to drive?"

Fred didn't answer right away. Finally with a wry smile, he said slowly, "You're doing fine, boy. Just keep going."

That's the nicest thing he's ever said to me!

"Why did you call me Joey?" Ben asked.

"Huh?" Fred looked startled.

"Before. When you were woozy."

When Fred didn't answer, Ben glanced over at him. He looked shaken.

After a polite interval, he asked, "Who's Joey?"

Fred looked out the side window. After a long time, he said, "Joey was my boy. He…." There was another long pause. "He and his mother were hit by a drunk driver. He was nine. They both died."

Ben didn't know what to say. "I…I…I'm sorry," he stuttered. "That's awful."

After more silence and a long sigh, Fred spoke. "I tried to forget. It hurt too much. Then you came to the ranch. You always reminded me of him."

He sniffed hard and cleared his throat. "I hated you for it. I hated you for reminding me all over again. I didn't want you around."

A stab of pain tore through Ben's chest. He could hardly see the road through his blurry eyes.

Now I get it. Boy, have I misjudged poor old Fred.

"I said a lot of mean stuff to you," Fred admitted, still looking out the window. "I guess I'm just a mean, rotten, old man."

"No, you're not!" Ben exclaimed. For some strange reason he felt like defending Fred.

Keeping his eyes on the muddy road, he said sheepishly, "I gave you plenty of reasons to get mad. It seems like whatever I do, I manage to cause a disaster."

Fred pointed out the window. "Watch out for that hole!"

Ben steered around it.

"Well, you're doing a heck of a job herding this rig down the mountain. For a kid, I mean."

Ben couldn't hold back a grin. Somehow, all the anger and bitterness he had built up against Fred melted away. In its place he felt an awkward closeness to the old man.

"Oh, shoot," Ben said. "Here's another one."

A little more confidently than before, he maneuvered cleanly around another switchback. As they dropped in elevation, the snow turned to sleet, then rain—they were almost to the valley floor. The heavy gray clouds hovered just above them.

By the time they hit blacktop, they had left the storm behind on the mountain. Breathing a prayer of thanks, Ben suddenly understood why God had let all this happen.

He pulled the rig to a stop, got out, and turned the hubs back to two-wheel drive. Starting up again, he shifted smoothly into first, then second, then third. Now they could make some time, and it was only a few miles to the ranch.

"Put the spurs to her, kid," Fred urged. "I ain't feeling so hot, you know."

Ben pulled in at the bunkhouse and ran inside. Seth was the only one up and about. Quickly Ben filled him in on the situation.

"I'll drive him to Elko," Seth said, reaching for his hat and jacket. "I'm feeling good enough."

"I want to go too," Ben said firmly. "Just stop by my house real quick so I can tell my mom."

Ben slid to the middle of the pickup seat next to Fred and Seth got behind the wheel. When they pulled up in front of Ben's house, Susie came out to meet them.

"What are you doing back already?"

"Mom! Fred's hurt! We're taking him to Elko!"

"Oh dear!" Apparently it didn't occur to her to ask how they got home. "Here, take our truck! It's got a full tank of gas. I'll take that truck over to the barn and unload the horses."

"Hey, thanks a lot, Susie!" Seth said. "We need to hightail it out of here!"

They switched trucks, helping Fred get comfortable. Once on the highway, Seth ignored the speed limit, flying down the long empty stretch of road leading to Elko.

"Now, tell me what happened," he said.

Ben looked at Fred, who shrugged.

"You tell," he grunted. "My head's still fuzzy."

Ben began with the cat tracks he had seen near camp. There was no need to tell all the stuff about the arguments, and the part about Joey was too private to tell right now.

Somehow, by the time he had narrated the day's events, Ben didn't feel nearly as sick about it as he had earlier. Talking about it seemed to help. So did the approving comments from Seth about how he had handled things.

When he finished, Seth grinned his slow grin and drawled, "Well, it doesn't sound like old Bad-news Ben made such a bad showing today!"

Mortified, Ben glanced at Fred out of the corner of his eye, then back at Seth. Seth leaned around Ben to stare right at Fred, saying pointedly, "Now did he, Fred?"

Now Fred looked embarrassed. "Like I told the boy," he growled, "I've said some stuff I shouldn't have. Hey, he did a man's job today. I ain't got no quarrel with him."

Ben's chest felt like fireworks were going off inside him. Maybe now was the time to say his piece about the money.

But just then, Fred reached up and turned the rearview mirror so he could see himself, bloody handkerchief and all. He fingered the orange twine and snorted.

"Where the heck did you get this?"

Ben winced. "It's all I could find. It's been in my pocket since the day I..." His voice trailed off into an awkward silence.

Fred's eyes narrowed. He stared at Ben without speaking. Ben got more and more uncomfortable. The easy feeling he had toward Fred evaporated.

A partly-suppressed chuckle broke the silence.

Next thing Ben knew, Fred let out a guffaw. Wincing, he reached for his head. "Oh, that hurts!"

Ben's eyes got big, and he just looked at Fred. Fred grinned weakly, and Seth began laughing. Then Ben began to laugh too. Seth slapped Ben on the leg, and they laughed until tears ran down their faces. Seth had to slow the truck down.

Fred just sat there with his eyes closed, holding his head. "Shut up and drive!" he said. "You're making my danged old head hurt!"

Ben sobered up as he thought of what he needed to say. "Uh, Fred, I've been needing to talk to you about that money. You know, for that horse."

Fred looked at him but didn't say anything.

"I don't want it to come out of my dad's pay. It's my responsibility. I have a little in the bank, and I tried to earn the rest, but..."

He stopped, took a deep breath, and plunged on to the hard part. "I've got about $500. For the other thousand, I'll have to give you my colt, Soapsuds. I hope that's enough."

There. He'd said it.

No one said anything.

Ben held his breath. In the very back of his mind was the dim hope that Fred, for some crazy reason, might not accept his offer.

Finally Fred spoke. "I've seen your colt, son. He's a double-good son-of-a-gun." He paused.

Ben held on to his tiny hope. *Please, God.*

"I don't need a bill of sale," Fred said. "A man's word is good enough for me. Let's shake on it." He held out his hand.

Hope died away, but was replaced by a small warm glow. Twice now Fred had referred to him as a man. Sort of. In a round-about way. A man who had taken responsibility for his actions. He grasped Fred's gnarled old hand and gave a firm shake.

"It's a done deal," Fred said, nodding with approval. "Your dad raised you to be a fine young man. He ought to be right proud. If I had a boy, I'd want him to be like you." His eyes met Ben's, and Ben gulped as he again felt that stab in his chest.

Seth clapped Ben on the leg. "There. You see? I guess you're not plumb useless after all. You'd better watch out, or old Fred'll be putting you to work, expecting you to do a man's job every day!"

Ben laughed, grateful that Seth had lightened the mood.

"Hey, we're here!" he said with relief, as they slowed down for the speed zone at the edge of Elko.

In no time, they were helping Fred into the emergency room. It turned out that Fred wasn't in any great danger, but since he lived so far away, the doctor wanted him to stay a day or two so he could keep an eye on him. Suspecting a concussion or fracture, he wanted to do a CT scan.

The cut needed stitching, and the doctor ordered a tetanus shot. Seth and Ben helped the nurse turn Fred onto his stomach. They politely looked the other way as she uncovered his bottom. But when they heard her say, "Hmmm," they saw that she was having trouble getting the needle to go in.

She gasped. "Oops! Oh, I'm so sorry! I've broken the needle! Let me get another one and try again." She broke the second one too. Seth and Ben teased Fred about having a hide like leather, but the nurse was beside herself with embarrassment, apologizing over and over.

Fred grinned and said, "You're just used to shooting them fluffy-butted city boys!"

They left Fred complaining about the IV stuck in his arm and the stupid nightgown he wore.

Pulling into the ranch well after dark, they saw that the cattle had arrived home. The light was on in the barn and Pete was inside, brushing down his tired horse. After leaving Ben and the truck at the barn, Seth headed for the bunkhouse.

"Hey there!" Pete said. "I wondered where you guys were."

"Dad, you'll never guess what happened today!"

"Where's Fred?" Pete interrupted.

"He's in the hospital in Elko. Seth and I just got back. That's what I mean!"

"What? What happened?"

"Oh, Dad, this has been the worst day of my whole life!" He quickly summarized the day's events, including the deal he'd made with Fred.

When he finished, his dad looked at him for a long time, his blue eyes warm and soft. He sniffed, then swallowed hard. Grabbing Ben's shoulder, he said gruffly, "You did good. I'm real proud of you, son."

Ben's chest felt like exploding and he stood a little taller. *Maybe this hasn't been the worst day of my life.* Strangely, it almost felt like it might be the best day of his life. Even losing Soapsuds didn't hurt so much right now.

He and his dad got in the truck and went home to rehearse the story once more. Ben didn't tell his parents the part about Joey; that could wait until later. Right now it was a bond between him and Fred that he didn't feel like sharing with anyone, not even Seth.

Early Sunday evening, Ben finished the riata. He and Skeeter hurried out to saddle up two horses in the fading daylight, and tested it on a few leppy calves in a pen down by the barn. Skeeter caught every one on the first try.

"Hey, this thing is hot!" he exclaimed. "You did alright!"

Ben grinned. His hands itched to try it out.

"You ever roped with a riata?" Skeeter asked, coiling it up neatly. Ben shook his head. "Here, give it a try." He rode over and handed it to Ben.

Ben took his reins and the coiled riata in his left hand above his horse's neck, feeding out enough rope to build a loop with his right hand. Swinging it slowly over his head, he picked out a small calf and guided his horse into position with his legs.

The big loop hummed as he rotated his wrist. Taking aim, he let go of the loop, opening his left fingers to release the coils. The loop flew through the air with uncanny accuracy.

It landed on the calf's hip, setting an open trap like a snare for the calf to step into. As Ben lifted his right hand high, the loop tightened. He took two quick dallies around the horn.

Just as Skeeter had said, the riata felt alive, like holding a rattlesnake. Ben delighted in the feel of the riata he had made with his own hands.

Skeeter cheered. "Yee-haw! Nailed him! Now drag him to the fire!"

Laughing, Ben pretended he was taking the calf to the branding fire. As he turned his horse, he let the dallies slide on his horn and dragged the calf across the pen.

"I'm gonna make one of these for myself!" Ben said with enthusiasm as he swung his horse around to face the calf. Lifting the rope straight up with his right hand, he popped his dallies, and the calf stepped out of the loop. He coiled up the riata and handed it back to Skeeter.

Monday, Seth brought Fred home from Elko. A few minutes after Pete came in for supper, Fred showed up at the kitchen door, carrying a package.

Ben opened the door. "Come on in." He looked at his dad with a question in his eyes.

"Hey, Fred, I owe you an apology," Pete said awkwardly. "What I said at the cabin...I had no business shooting off my mouth like that."

"Forget it," Fred said. "If we didn't have that argument, you'd never have sent Ben back with me. I might still be lying up there—just an old dead, frozen cowboy."

Pete nodded, grinning. They shook hands.

"I guess that storm's dumped a bunch of snow up there," Pete said. "Good thing we got those cows out. How you feeling?"

"Well, they didn't have to amputate my head, so I guess it's okay." Everyone laughed.

After a pause, Fred said in a gruff voice, "Here," shoving the package toward Ben. "Open it."

Ben tore the wrapping off, opened the box and pulled out a big glossy orange scarf.

"I figger'd you needed a nice colorful wildrag, if you're going to be buckarooing."

Ben grabbed two diagonal corners and wrapped it twice around his neck. He started to tie the ends in a square knot like his dad did.

"You better tie yours in a slipknot, boy," Fred said drily. "Knowing you, you're liable to get it caught on a branch when you're riding. A slipknot'll jerk loose."

He cleared his throat. Sounding almost embarrassed, he added, "Don't want you to hang up or nothing."

Laughing, Ben tied the shiny orange wildrag in a slipknot.

Yep, a true buckaroo. That's what I want to be.

He took his black felt hat off the hat rack and placed it on his head. With a tug on the brim, he pulled it down low over his eyes and stepped over to the mirror to admire himself. He grinned.

"Thanks, Fred!"

RANCHING TERMS & COWBOY SLANG

alfalfa — A leafy green crop often grown for hay. To turn alfalfa into hay, it must be cut, partly dried, and made into bales.

ATV — All Terrain Vehicle, also known as a four-wheeler or a quad.

bag balm — Lanolin ointment for cows' udders, also frequently used for human and animal cuts and sores.

bale — Hay that has been compressed and tied into a rectangular shape. Regular bales, or small bales, are about four feet long and may weigh from 80 pounds to 130 pounds. Big bales can be about six feet long and weigh about a ton. There are also big round bales.

baler — A tractor-like machine or a machine pulled by a tractor, that picks up the cut and dried alfalfa, forms it into bales, and ties it with twine or wire.

bale wagon or harobed (pronounced "HARROW-bed") —A machine for picking up rectangular bales from the field and stacking them. Harobed is the name of the inventor's daughter spelled backward (Deborah).

Basque — (pronounced "bask") A descendant of a population group from the Pyrennees mountains, on the border of France and Spain, many of whom settled in the intermountain West and became active in the sheep and cattle industries.

bay — A reddish-brown horse with black legs and black mane and tail (also referred to as black points).

blister — Derogatory term, as in "the old blister." A blister is sensitive, touchy, sore. The connotation is "grouchy."

border collie — A breed of dogs used for working cattle or sheep; usually black with white ring around neck, white tip on tail, and other white markings.

bosal — A true hackamore, as opposed to a mechanical hackamore. It consists of a braided nose band, usually of rawhide, hung from a light headstall (called a hanger), with a heel knot under the horse's chin where the mecate reins (usually horsehair) are attached. Bosal may refer to just the nose band, or the entire set-up. The bosal is generally the training stage between the snaffle and the bit.

brand — An identifying mark put on cattle or horses. It is applied quickly with a hot branding iron, leaving a permanent mark on the skin. Each ranch not only has its own registered brand, but a particular location for its brand—left shoulder, right hip, left side, etc.

bridle — A piece of equipment made of leather straps that go over the horse's head and hold the bit in the horse's mouth. The reins are attached to the bit.

buckaroo — Cowboy; from the Spanish term *vaquero*. A term most commonly used in the intermountain region of the West (mainly California, Nevada, southern Idaho, eastern Oregon). *Vaca* means "cow" in Spanish; *vaquero* means "cow-worker." *Vaquero* became "bukera" (buh-KER-uh), then "buckaroo."

build a loop — To build a loop in a lass rope, you hold the coiled rope in your left hand, and with your right hand on the hondoo, turn and shake out the end with the hondoo to make that coil into a bigger loop. With a flick of your right wrist, you turn it and whip the rope, feeding out coils with your left hand, so more rope slides through the hondoo until you have a loop the size you want.

bull — A male member of the cattle (bovine) family. A mature female is a cow; a young female is a heifer. A young male is a calf, but calf can refer to any young bovine, male or female. Plural of calf is calves.

bunkhouse — A ranch building where single cowboys live.

cayuse — (pronounced "KIY-yoos") Horse. From the name of an Indian tribe; hence, originally the idea of an Indian pony.

center pivot — An irrigation system consisting of long segments of pipe supported on towers with wheels. The water flows through the pipe and out through sprinklers attached at intervals to the underneath side of the pipe as the whole thing pivots around a central point, watering a circular field.

chaps — (pronounced "shaps") From the Spanish term *chapareras* or *chaparajos*. Leather leggings worn over jeans, to protect the legs and clothing from brush, often with fringe along the edge. Full-length chaps are called shotguns, and are worn mainly in cold weather. In warm weather, cowboys often wear short chaps, called chinks, which come to the knee or below. Chaps also give the rider a more secure seat in the saddle; leather leggings against a leather saddle are not as slippery as jeans against leather.

Charlie Russell — A famous Western artist/cowboy of the 1800's whose paintings, drawings, and sculptures accurately depicted cowboy life.

chin strap — A short strap that goes loosely behind the horse's chin, from one end of the bit to the other. Sometimes a small, fine chain is used.

cinch — From the Spanish word *cincha,* meaning belt. The cloth or webbed band that goes around the horse's belly to hold the saddle in place with large rings on each end that the latigos are attached to. Some saddles also have a back cinch, a wide leather strap attached to the saddle just behind the stirrups. This helps stabilize the saddle, especially when roping a cow.

cleanup — The last trip up into the mountains before winter to gather the few cattle missed in the main fall cattle drive.

colt — A young horse, especially one that is not yet fully trained. A horse is considered mature around 5-7 years of age, by which time it is no longer referred to as a colt. Also may refer technically to a young male horse, whereas a young female is a filly.

cow boss — The head cowboy on a ranch employing a number of cowboys, somewhat like a foreman. If the ranch also engages in farming and employs farm help, there might also be a farm boss. They would report to the owner, or if the ranch is run by a ranch manager, to that person.

cow camp — A primitive one-room cabin in the mountains or out in the desert, far from the ranch headquarters but located on its leased public land, where one or more cowboys may stay for periods of time. It may also have a set of corrals. Many ranches have an "open door policy" on their cow camps: anyone in the area may stay in them in a pinch, provided they replace the supplies and firewood they use.

crowhop — A mild form of bucking, usually a series of little short jumps, not hard to ride. Instead of kicking the hind feet up and out, the feet stay down, the head goes down, and the back is arched.

cutting (of alfalfa hay) — When alfalfa is swathed (cut) to be made into hay, it is partly dried, raked once to turn it over for even drying, then baled, removed from the field, and stored in a stack in a stackyard. That is one cutting of hay. The alfalfa plants are watered, continue to grow, and 4-6 weeks later, are again swathed, raked, baled, and stacked. That is another cutting of hay. In cold climates and high elevations, 2-3 cuttings are common in one growing season. In warmer, lower climates, 8-10 cuttings are possible.

day work — Hiring out to work on a day-by-day basis rather than for a monthly salary.

dally — From the Spanish *de la vuelta* meaning "to turn around." To go around the saddle horn with a rope one or more times. Because the rope isn't tied down hard and fast, the dallies can be "slipped" on the horn for easier and more humane handling of cattle.

flake (of hay) — When alfalfa is mechanically fed into a baler, the baler's plunger compresses the hay each time it takes a stroke. Each stroke forms a tightly packed chunk of hay—a flake. When the bale is broken open for feeding, it can be easily pulled apart in flakes, each about four inches thick.

flesh — To scrape away the fatty, fleshy layer on the inside of a hide that has been stretched and dried.

fork — To straddle a horse; your legs are like the tines of a fork on each side. A cowboy that can stay in the saddle no matter how rank the horse is considered pretty "fork-ed," pronounced as two syllables.

gelding — A male horse that has been castrated, a process in which the sex glands are removed. Colts are generally gelded by the age of two. A gelding has a calmer, more even disposition than a stud (an intact male, also called a stallion, used for breeding and sometimes for riding).

gooseneck trailer — A stock trailer with a front end that extends over the pickup bed. Its hitch attaches in the middle of the bed, over the axle. Because of this arrangement, it pulls better than bumper-pull trailers. Most are big enough to hold four or more horses or cows.

ground squirrel — The Belding's ground squirrel (*Spermophilus beldingi*) and Townsend's ground squirrel (*Spermophilus townsendii*) are found in Nevada: Mammal, Order Rodentia, Family Sciuridae, Genus *Spermophilus*. Often referred to as a gopher, this rodent is smaller than its relative, the prairie dog. It is considered a destructive pest in agricultural areas because of its burrowing activity.

gunsel — A useless, inept, no-account, or "wanna-be" cowboy.

halter — A loose bitless headgear of rope or leather, to which a lead rope can be attached, so that a horse may be led or tied.

halter break — To put a halter on a horse and teach it to accept being led and tied up. The horse generally struggles against the rope until it realizes it cannot gain its freedom by pulling against the rope. Once a horse has been halter broke, it can be led or tied.

hand — Someone who's pretty good help, particularly around a ranch or with a horse. Examples: "He'll never make a hand," or, "He's a pretty fair hand with a horse."

A hand is also a unit of measure—four inches. Horses are measured in hands, not feet or inches. Their height is measured at the withers, the bony hump where the neck meets the back at the top of the shoulder blades. For example, the size range of the average ranch horse might be: 15, 15-1, 15-2, 15-3, 16.

harobed — See bale wagon.

hay — Partly dried grass or alfalfa that is usually formed into bales for long-term storage.

haying — The process of growing and harvesting hay (grass or alfalfa—usually in the form of bales) and storing it to feed to horses and cattle later.

headstall — The part of a bridle consisting of leather straps that go over and around the horse's head; it does not include the bit or reins.

hightail — To go in a big hurry, as calves run and buck with their tails high in the air.

hobbles — A heavy leather strap that goes around the horse's front legs below the knees in a figure-eight, then is buckled snugly. Hobbles keep the horse from traveling very far or fast, and are used when there is no place to tie a horse, or to allow the horse to graze while being restrained. Also called a set of hobbles.

hondoo — From the Spanish term *hondo* meaning "deep." Also called hondo or honda. A metal, plastic or braided leather oblong ring at the end of a rope through which the rope is passed to make a loop. It may also be a loop braided into the end of the rope.

lass rope — Another word for lasso. More often just called a rope. Buckaroos generally refer to it as a rope or lass rope; Texas cowboys are more apt to say lasso.

lasso (pronounced "lass-sue") — From the Spanish term *lazo,* meaning "length of line." A particular type of stiff narrow rope used for roping animals. A large loop is formed, swung, and thrown over the head or around the feet. Also called lariat, from the Spanish, *la riata,* meaning "the rope." Lasso and lariat are terms seldom used by buckaroos.

latigo — From the Spanish term *latigo* meaning "the whip." A long leather strap that attaches the cinch ring to the rigging ring on each side of a western saddle.

The cinch hangs from the right latigo. To cinch up, the left latigo is wrapped snugly several times and either buckled or tied.

lead rope — A rope attached to the halter for leading and tying.

leppy — A calf that has lost its mother, which causes it to do poorly. When applied to a person, the connotation is "useless" or "sorry."

loading chute — A narrow ramp with sides, slanting upward, used for loading cattle into trucks. Some are built into a set of corrals, and some are portable.

lope — Gallop. Western riders seldom use the terms gallop or canter, although these all refer to the same basic gait. Lope may imply a relaxed gallop. A fast gallop might be called a hard lope or a dead run.

mare — A female horse, especially a mature female.

mother up — Calves get separated from their mothers while being worked or driven. When they are left alone, the mothers begin noisily looking through the herd for their calves, eventually reuniting. This process is called "mothering up."

mucho dinero — (pronounced "MOO-cho de-NAIR-o") — Spanish for "much money."

on the hook — A cow that is "on the hook" is mad, slinging her horns to try to hook someone or something. When applied to a person, the connotation is "mad."

onry — Ornery.

pencil-neck — A neck as skinny as a pencil implies lack of muscle, no experience with hard work. The connotation is "wimpy."

pocket gophers — Pocket gophers are often confused with squirrels or prairie dogs. The species of pocket gopher found in northern Nevada is Townsend's pocket gopher *(Thomomys townsendii)*: Mammal, Order Rodentia, Family geomyidae, Genus *Thomomys* (western pocket gopher). This mammal lives almost entirely underground. Considered a destructive pest in agricultural areas, it can be useful in open areas by aiding soil formation through "rototilling" of the soil. Mounds can catch blowing seeds to begin new plant life.

public lands — When Nevada became a state, Congress attached a condition. Nevada must give up ownership of all land which was not privately owned at that time—87% of Nevada's land. Although controlled by the government, this land is for public use. For the first 70 years of Nevada's statehood, it was free grazing land. But problems developed. Some stockmen put too many animals on the range and let them overgraze it. The federal government stepped in to solve these problems.

In 1934 the Taylor Grazing Act was passed. Grazing districts were established. Rules and regulations followed. Ranchers had to apply for grazing permits and pay grazing fees. Grazing permits are handled by the U.S. Forest Service and the BLM (Bureau of Land Management). These agencies limit the number and type of livestock on each allotment and the length of time they can graze there.

The BLM, which was formed in 1947, manages 261 million acres of public lands which are located mostly in 12 western states. Today there is much controversy over the use of public lands by ranchers. Some ecologists and government bureaucrats say cattle damage public lands. Ranchers claim they can't afford to raise cattle without the use of public lands. Studies show that grazing actually improves the health of rangelands.

punchy — Overdressed to appear buckaroo-ish.

put down — Put to sleep, put out of its misery, or euthanize with a gun or a veterinarian's needle.

Queensland heeler — A type of cowdog from the Queensland area of Australia.

rawhide — Untanned cowhide.

read a cow — Know what a cow is thinking and what it's likely to do next.

riata — From the Spanish term *la riata,* meaning "the rope." Also spelled "reata." A lasso made of braided rawhide, generally 65-80 feet long. Often used in the intermountain region where the Spanish vaquero influence is still felt (mainly California, Nevada, southern Idaho, eastern Oregon).

snaffle/snaffle bit — A snaffle bit is a mild jointed bit that works on the corners of the horse's lips rather than the inside of the mouth. It is generally used on young horses, before they are introduced to a bit, and is generally used with two hands on the reins. A bit works on the mouth, has shanks on the side that exert leverage, and is used one-handed. A horse that goes in a bit is said to be "in the bridle." A horse may be "started in the bridle," or if it well-trained and responsive to the bridle, is said to be "bridled," "straight up in the bridle," "finished" or is referred to as a "bridle horse." Many cowboys routinely ride their horses in the snaffle, regardless of the horse's age or stage of training, because it is so easy on the mouth. When talking about types of bits, "bit" does not refer to the snaffle, but rather a leverage bit. However, if you are putting the snaffle in the horse's mouth, you would say you are putting the bit in his mouth.

sorrel — A reddish-orange horse, usually with mane and tail of the same color as its coat.

sourdough — A dough that is leavened with a homemade yeast, which keeps for long periods of time. When used regularly, sourdough starter can be kept going for many years. Before each use, it must set in a warm place overnight to activate the yeast. Sourdough hotcakes have a light yeasty flavor. Once known as the mainstay of chuck wagon cooks in the old West, it is still used for its unique flavor.

sow — (rhymes with "how") Female pig or hog. When applied to a female horse or cow, the connotation could be "hoggish" or "snotty." May also be used casually of any female horse or cow.

spooky — Describes a horse that spooks easily--that startles or jumps at any little noise, movement, or unusual object.

spurs — From the Spanish term *la espuela*. Metal prods strapped to the heel of the boot. They vary from short to long. They usually have a rowel—a spinning disk with sharp or dull points. Spurs are often inlaid with silver, and spur straps are often stamped with intricate designs.

stock saddle — A large, heavy, western-style saddle used for working livestock.

stock trailer — A trailer for hauling livestock, usually larger than the common two-horse trailer.

swather — A piece of farm equipment used for cutting hay. It may be a tractor-like machine with cutting blades on the front, or it may be an implement pulled behind a tractor.

tanning — A process by which animal skin is turned into leather and preserved by applying a substance called tannin.

.30-30 — A commonly used rifle, often a lever-action, more powerful than the .22. (pronounced "thirty-thirty")

tie rack — Hitching rail.

trap — A fenced area for temporarily holding or working cattle. It might even just be a "V" in a fence, not enclosed on all sides. It can be temporarily enclosed by parking pickups and trailers along the open side, or stringing rope.

.22 — A commonly used small caliber rifle. (pronounced "twenty-two")

white-faced cattle — A common term for Hereford cattle, which are red with white faces. They are raised for beef.

wildrag — A large neckerchief or scarf of shiny, silky material, usually at least three feet square. It is folded in half from two farthest corners, forming a triangle, then wrapped twice around the neck and tied in a knot. It is a common item of buckaroo clothing, especially in cold weather.

To order copies of *The Orange Slipknot,*
or other Raven Publishing novels, please complete
the order form on the next page.
Mail the order form with payment to:

Raven Publishing, Inc.
PO Box 2866, Norris, MT 59745

or order online at:
www.ravenpublishing.net

To view details of our books see our website
or call our toll-free number for a free catalog.

Comprehensive cross-curriculum units are available
for *The Orange Slipknot, Miranda and Starlight,*
and *Starlight's Courage* for using these books in
classrooms and home schools.
Please contact us for special pricing
and more information.

Phone: 866-685-3545   Fax: 406-685-3599
email: info@ravenpublishing.net

Quantity	Title	Price	Total
_____	The Orange Slipknot	$10.00	_____
_____	Miranda and Starlight, Revised Edition	$9.00	_____
_____	Starlight's Courage, Revised Edition	$9.00	_____
_____	Starlight, Star Bright	$9.00	_____
_____	Starlight's Shooting Star	$9.00	_____
_____	Starlight Shines for Miranda	$9.00	_____
_____	Starlight Comes Home	$9.00	_____
_____	Starlight series, six book Gift Set	$54.00	_____
_____	Fergus, The Soccer-Playing Colt	$9.00	_____
_____	An Inmate's Daughter	$9.00	_____
_____	Absaroka	$10.00	_____
_____	Danny's Dragon	$10.00	_____
_____	A Horse to Remember	$10.00	_____
	Subtotal		_____
	Shipping		_____
	Total:		_____

Add $3.00 Shipping and handling for the first book
and $.50 for each additional book.

Please fill out shipping and payment information

Ship to:

Name_____

Address_____

City_____State_____Zip_____

Billing:

_____Check or money order enclosed

_____Visa _____MasterCard _____Discover

Name on Credit Card_____

Billing address _____

City _____State_____ Zip_____

Account Number_____

Expiration Date_____mm/yy

Security Code _____

Total amount (from other side) _____

Send to:

Raven Publishing, Inc.
P.O. Box 2866
Norris, MT 59745